OVER EASY

Books by Kathryn Elizabeth Jones

A River of Stones

Parable Series

Conquering Your Goliaths: A Parable of the Five Stones
Conquering Your Goliaths: Guidebook
The Feast: A Parable of the Ring
The Gift: A Parable of the Key

Heaven 24/7

Living in the Light
with M. Celeste Martin

Marketing Your Book on a Budget

Susan Cramer Mysteries

Scrambled
Sunny Side-Up
Hard Boiled
Over Easy

OVER EASY

A Susan Cramer Mystery

Book 4

KATHRYN ELIZABETH JONES

Idea Creations Press
www.ideacreationspress.com

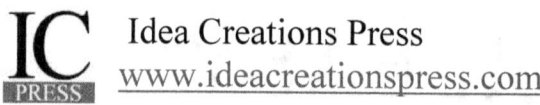
Idea Creations Press
www.ideacreationspress.com

Library of Congress Control Number: 2017905043

ISBN-13: 9780997890433
ISBN-10: 0997890436

Printed in the U.S.A.

Acknowledgments

This book is dedicated to my wise and faithful beta readers: Bethany Wursten, Tricia Leslie, and Carolyn Tolman and to my many mystery readers - you know who you are. Thank you!

Preface

Susan reached for the wooden pumpkin on the Halloween display. Her daughter, Brianne, had encouraged her to come, or rather, forced her to take part in the venture by her relentless whining. Susan decided the trip would be bearable when Jane Dove, her friend and current manager of *Honesty House*, had decided to tag along.

With Halloween music playing over the PA system, and plenty of people talking and drooling over the numerous treasures at the yearly craft fair, it was no surprise that her daughter would get in on the act, though a sudden squeal made Susan jump.

"Mom! You won't believe this!" Brianne picked up a wicked looking witch — green face and all, including the curled toes and long red fingernails. The thing was made of varying fabrics; at least that's what it looked like from one booth away.

Jane smiled over at her.

"Now, don't you two go getting any ideas! We'll look at everything, and then come back later when we've decided on what we want," Susan said.

"Oh, you're no fun." Brianne poised the witch in front of her. "What do you think, Wicked?" she asked.

"You or the witch?" Susan couldn't help asking.

"Oh, Mom!"

At 15, 'Oh Mom' was about as popular as 'you just don't get it,' and frankly, Susan would need some good old rest when she finally managed to tuck herself in bed.

Of course, there was Henry, would always be Henry, but Henry often made it to bed before she did, wrapping himself in the old quilt for warmth. The thing had hung on the quilt rack for the entire summer, but now that the weather was cooling down, it was the quilt that would settle him even before she'd made it to bed.

Near thirty minutes later, a screech the size of Texas enveloped her ears, and Susan couldn't help but stop and listen. This time it didn't come from her daughter, at least not that she could tell. She could no longer see Brianne up the aisle looking over the witch decoration. The sound appeared to have come from the far corner of the room. They were indoors, in an old farm building rented out for just such occasions. Craft shows would never be her cup of tea, but then again, if coming to them meant she had more time with her friend and daughter, so be it.

A clamoring of people passed her and she set the pumpkin down on the table. Susan turned, searching the aisle with her eyes. The spooky Halloween music, fit for such an occasion as this, had suddenly stopped. In its place, howling. Was someone — crying?

She looked up but didn't see her daughter. "Brianne?" she called through the crowd.

Jane took her by the arm. "I think the sound came from over here," she said, yanking Susan in the direction of the back door — the one that led customers to door number two where even more treasures would be displayed.

They were forced to stop suddenly, as heads were all they could see in the gathering crowd. "What do you think happened?" Susan asked, stunned at the amount of traffic that could find a screech so interesting in just a matter of seconds.

Jane shook her head. "I have no idea. Where is Brianne?"

Susan shrugged, turned briefly and then back to see a woman's face directly in front of her. The dark headed woman with blue eyes blinked. "I think someone's dead," she said.

***

As the ambulance arrived, the crowd parted, only to reveal a young woman — probably in her early-twenties — lying motionless on the cement floor. Crusted blood issued from the right side of her head and her hand lay bloody on the floor. A black shoe — a stiletto — was lying next to her head and she wore a black party dress. Her hair was a long silky black. She wasn't moving and her chest wasn't rising, at least not that Susan could determine from five feet away.

She still hadn't seen her daughter. And Jane? Susan was worried.

She searched the crowd. So many people and where was the other shoe?

"Everyone, stand back!" someone shouted, and in moments she was being pushed back along with the others.

"Mom! Mom!" Brianne yelled, fighting her way through the crowd.

"Brianne! Thank heavens you're alright!"

"I... was just talking to her," she returned, her words stumbling. "She said... she said that she needed to use the restroom. And she left me. I... "

Susan wrapped her arm around Brianne's shoulder, squeezing it tightly. So, it was happening again, the death magnet. She would never understand death's attraction to her if she lived to be a million years old. "Look, there are the police," she said.

"The po -lice?" Brianne gasped. The girl shook.

"Did you see the killer?" Susan asked, mortified at the crowd following the dead woman out; she'd been placed on a gurney.

Jane was suddenly beside her. She took Brianne by the other arm. "You're as white as a sheet. Let's find you a chair."

Brianne nodded and followed them clumsily to a bench just outside the door. Susan held her daughter close as she watched the gurney slide into the back end of the ambulance. The doors shut, the eerie shrill of the siren met her ears.

"Oh, Mom!"

"Yes?"

"Who would want to kill *her*? I mean, she was so nice. She talked to me like we were – old friends. She was dressed up, 'ready to go to a party,' she said. I might have said only ten words to her, and then she excused herself. About twenty minutes later, I heard a scream. I couldn't find you."

"Sorry. I was doing what everyone else was doing," she said.

Jane shook her head. "Where were you anyway?"

"Around the corner."

"Did you see anything?" Susan asked, for again, it occurred to her that Brianne might have been within eyeshot of the murder – the girl was definitely dead from the looks of things. As she was placed in the ambulance there was nothing to assist with breathing, just a sheet over the body.

"I'm not sure." Brianne shifted uneasily on her chair. "I mean, her head was down a little, she seemed to be looking at some clothing closer to the floor. I looked down myself to check something out and when I heard the scream I looked up. I don't know how I knew, but I knew it was her."

A creepy feeling crept up Susan's back.

"I couldn't move. People raced past me to the area where I'd last seen her standing, but I could no longer see her. I hoped I couldn't see her because of the crowd, but when I finally found you and the... I figured it had to be her."

"Who is she?"

"I don't know... I mean, Roxanne. Her name is Roxanne. She's older than I am, though she didn't tell me that. I figured she must be at Lowell or something. She had this cool pin on her purse and I complimented her on it: Rowan Halls."

"A sorority?" Jane asked.

Brianne nodded. "Gads, I don't think I can shop anymore," she said.

***

Henry was not happy. As they sat with their daughter at police headquarters, all Susan could think about were the cases before this one that she had bungled. But maybe, this time, all it would take would be a short confession about what her daughter had seen and then they could go about their merry way. There was always hope.

Henry wasn't well, but he sat there with the two of them. Henry's detective agency wasn't going so well and most days he simply didn't have the energy to help Jane over at *Honesty House*. Susan knew it was his heart. She knew it, and it killed her to know that Henry might never quite be himself again. After numerous visits to the hospital — numerous tests and heart procedures, Henry's heart was failing, and he had been put on a transplant list.

Still, when it came to his son — currently in school, a spit-fire of a kid who now appeared to like girls for none of the important reasons — Henry wouldn't let his illness keep him from most things that concerned him. Oscar was 18, and thinking of attending Lowell, a local college, and driving them crazy with late nights and homework at 2 a.m. Oscar would graduate high school this year and Susan didn't even want to think about it.

"And where were you at the time of the stabbing?" Police Officer Crump asked.

"I don't know..." Brianne stumbled.

"What did you do after she left you?"

"I went back to looking at come other stuff... until I heard the scream."

"And you were standing — where?"

"Two booths down, around the corner from my mother and her friend, I was looking at some lotions and stuff — you know they make a thing called bath bombs that you can throw in your bath water and everything fizzes up?"

Police Officer Crump grunted. "I'm not sure I have," he said.

"You could get some for your wife," she offered.

"Not married. Should we get back to the questions?"

Brianne blushed. "Sorry," she said. "When I heard the scream, I looked up. I didn't see Roxanne anymore. There were a lot of people crowding in. I wondered what had happened."

"How much time do you think lapsed between Roxanne leaving you and hearing the scream?"

"Oh, I don't know. Maybe twenty minutes, but I'm not sure. I get really involved when I hunt for bargains."

Officer Crump stared wearily into Henry's eyes. "Haven't seen you for a while," he said. "How have you been?"

Henry blinked and then repeated the answer he'd given to everyone lately that had asked him that question. "A little tired, but not too worse for wear."

He sounded like an old man, though Susan would have never told Henry the same. Her love for him overcame all else. But the officer looked over at her now, a question on his tongue.

"And how are you, Susan? Do you know this Roxanne?"

"No. I've never met her, though my daughter says she must be attending a college somewhere..."

"We saw the sorority pin. An excellent observation," he added, turning again to Brianne who was deathly pale. "Anything else you noticed about the young woman that you'd like to tell me now?"

Susan could see her daughter's thoughts going deeper; could almost feel the fear Brianne must have experienced the moment she realized that Roxanne was dead. "Well, she was wearing black, as you probably already know. And she was beautiful. A black shoe was next to her hand. Where was the other one?" Brianne asked.

"We're not sure." He smiled. "She should have been wearing it."

If the officer had meant to be funny, the joke had fallen on less than eager ears.

"She had both shoes on when she talked with me. I couldn't believe how high they were — that she actually walked around the show in them. She said she was meeting her boyfriend later."

The officer wrote down some notes. "Anything else?"

"Let's see... I guess not."

Officer Crump wiped his bald head and stood. "Thank you. If I have any further questions, may I call you?"

"Just call me, I'll get the word on to Brianne," Henry offered before Brianne could speak. Brianne was underage after all, and the police would have to speak with she or Henry if any other information was needed.

Susan took Henry's hand. "Let's go," she said.

***

"So, how long have you known Crump?" Susan asked.

After returning home, Brianne had promptly gone to her room and shut the door behind her. Oscar was doing his homework in his room, though he'd managed a short 'hello' as they'd returned.

"I really don't," Henry answered, hanging his jacket on a hook near the door. Susan followed suit. In moments, they were sitting on the couch, he on one end, and she on the other. "Crump arrived just as I left. Transferred, I believe."

"Oh." Susan tried to smile but it just wasn't happening. Her husband looked so tired. He smiled over at her but his eyes weren't in it. "I'm sorry, Susan," he finally said, standing up and moving closer to her on the couch. "I feel like an old man."

"Well you're not," she said, placing her hands on his own. "You will always be my handsome husband."

"And you will always be my beautiful wife."

It was all too sentimental, Susan knew it, but they needed this time to talk, to think about something other than the inevitable. Susan couldn't think about the inevitable.

"Do you want to watch a movie?" she finally asked when neither of them seemed to have anything more to say.

OVER EASY

The Note

"Mom!" Brianne squealed. She was in the kitchen, and she was holding something. "Okay, so I should have told you, and maybe even the police, but I just couldn't."

"What?" Susan sat down at the table.

"Friend, I'm in trouble," it began. *"If you don't see me again, know that Rowan Halls has the answers. I'm afraid for my life — if we meet again, I'll tell you what I know. For now, I am being watched. Meet me at Greenfield tomorrow at 8 — that is, if I make it. Roxy."*

Brianne handed the paper to Susan.

The lined paper had words written in dark purple ink in a sort of flowing fashion, though there weren't any hearts for the 'I's'.

"Where did you get this?" Susan asked.

"Roxy. Oh, Mom, don't get mad. Maybe there is something we can figure out."

"Why didn't you tell the police yesterday?"

Brianne shrugged, though her skin was pale. "What's Greenfield?" she asked.

"Maybe a dorm on campus or a local hangout."

"That's what I thought."

"I'm taking this to the police. It's evidence."

"Sure, but do we have to?"

A shudder ran through Susan's body. "What do you mean, do we have to?"

"What if we don't tell them? Roxanne could have gone to the police but came to me instead."

"I know, and that's what I'm worried about."

"Oh, come on, Mom. Maybe it'll be fun. Maybe Roxy heard about you, about your detective work, and she was trying to find us so that she could get some help."

"Fine, but I'm taking this note to the police. Why would she give the note to you anyway?" she asked. The idea was ludicrous. Someone had actually searched her daughter out for help?

Brianne stood. Her light brown hair was pulled up into a twist. She wore an old yellow sweater and some leggings. Though her daughter was not a fashion queen by any sense of the word, it had always intrigued her how she could make something boring look suddenly put together.

"I don't know. Maybe she was just desperate for some help." She pulled on her coat, slinging on her backpack. "You can keep the note. Maybe you can read in-between the lines or something while I'm gone."

***

A day later, Susan still had the note. She handed it to Henry.

"Well, well," he began, looking up from the computer where he'd been working. "I wondered what would pop up. You are a death magnet you know."

"I know." She sat on the bed and looked at it. "But it's just a note, Henry. Come and see if you see anything."

Henry stood from the computer and slowly walked to her. Taking the piece of lined paper in his hands he began to read. "Well, you know what I'd do," he began, returning to the computer with the note.

"What?"

"Let me and Brianne take the note back to the police. They may have additional questions for her. You find this Greenfield place and see what's lurking behind the doors of Rowan Halls."

"And how am I supposed to do that?" Susan asked.

"Pretend you're a student."

She laughed. "You can't be serious," she said. She was in her late 40s after all. How could she pass off as a near 20-year-old?

He turned from the computer and looked at her — really looked at her this time.

"Susan, you know you've been aching to solve another mystery. And now, here is one that has fallen right into your lap."

"But a teenager, I..."

"No, you probably can't pose as a teenager, though beautiful you are, but your son can."

"Oscar?"

"Better than Brianne going, don't you think — you know how emotionally charged she gets. Why don't the two of you check out Rowan Halls — it will be a good front — maybe he'll like the college and want to go there next year. It couldn't hurt."

Susan smiled. The idea was brilliant, maybe too brilliant.

***

"I can't believe we're doing this."

"Believe it," said Susan, taking her son by the arm and leading them both into the building. "You need to attend this orientation eventually anyway."

"Yeah, but..."

Susan knew how he felt, or at least, thought she knew. The boy wanted to skip out on the orientation at all costs, primarily because it wasn't required, and weren't all the geeks attending? He wasn't a geek...

The brick building, housed multiple chairs in the main area, and a podium up front as well as a wide screen, probably for a PowerPoint presentation.

Oscar rolled his eyes and shifted uneasily in his chair. "What did Brianne think?" he asked.

"About what?"

"This little... venture. She's the one who wanted to be a part of this."

"The mystery? I know, but..."

"No 'butts' Mom, especially the big ones."

"What?"

"Never mind. They're starting."

The orientation for students who would be attending in the spring was long and winding, but when the speaker, a Miss Slack, got to Rowan

Halls and all of the other dorms available on campus, Susan's ears perked up. Oscar nudged her.

"For those of you starting after winter, rest assured that you'll want to have your name on the list. The time for moving into your new place will be here before you know it, and if your name is not on the list, well, you may not get in."

Susan wondered how many kids would 'get in' so to speak. There were hundreds in the room, their heads bobbing or sleeping next to a parent or friend. She knew that Oscar was ready to move out, but she wasn't sure that she wanted to let him."

"Of course, *Young*ston is the girl's dorm, the boys stay at Mc*Elderly*."

Laughter filled the room.

Oscar sniffed. "You'd think we were a bunch of old farts," he whispered into her ear.

"Shhh... I want to hear."

"*Youngston* is the most glamorous of homes." Miss Slack stared into the crowd and then at someone who must have been standing in the corner near the back of the room. Susan watched her eyes, as well as the boy she appeared to be staring at. He wore a heavy black coat, and his hair — blonde — stuck up in various spikes all over his head.

"I thought the spiked hair style was going out," she said.

"Who are you looking at?"

"That boy, there." She pointed. "See him?"

"Can't miss him."

"Do you know him?"

"No. Why?"

Susan turned her head to the front of the room. Miss Slack had just ended her rendition of *McElderly*, and the long distance between them. "We have strict rules, very strict rules here at Lowell. I expect everyone to remember that."

Susan looked back at the boy. He was smiling widely at the girl in front. *Probably girlfriend and boyfriend*, she thought. But people were standing — the meeting had ended.

"Get what you want?" Oscar offered.

"Some. What do you think "Greenfield" means?"

"You mean the cafeteria?"

Susan blinked at him.

"Everyone knows about Greenfield and its sometimes 'green' food, and I'm not talking about the lettuce. Like I said, we didn't need to come to this stupid orientation. I know all about this place."

Susan was dumbfounded. "Why didn't you say something. I would have..."

"You didn't ask." He offered her his arm. "Besides, coming to this boring meeting was a good opportunity to get some free lunch."

***

Susan was curious about the blonde headed boy, but more curious to check out the cafeteria. Hadn't Roxanne — the dead girl — say she wanted to meet Brianne here? Susan could only hope she'd discover something when they ordered their lunch.

Of course, there was nothing but new students and their parents walking around — for the most part — but the blonde-haired boy slipped in and out of the room like a ball outside a batting cage.

And then she saw her.

Oscar waved.

"Over here!" he yelled.

A few heads turned in their direction, including the boy with the spiky hair, and refreshing eyes blinked at her. "Hi, Mom," Brianne said, taking a seat with her tray already loaded. She'd chosen a sub sandwich, some chips, and a soda.

"That looks better than ours," said Oscar, scooting his tray of pizza to the side. "Wanna trade?"

"Forget it."

"So, did you learn anything?" She opened the bag of chips and began to chew.

Susan blinked. "What are you doing here?" she asked.

"The police were a little miffed at first, and asked me the same stuff. Nothing big. I convinced Dad I'd be a big help. He had stuff to do anyway and I was bored. He dropped me off. So, what have you found out?"

"Nothing much," Susan offered, looking over at her son for an apology. After all, he'd known all about Greenfield Cafeteria, who knew what else might be lurking around inside his teenaged brain. "Just about Rowan Halls. Roxanne must have lived there."

"I figured as much. And this place?"

"Just a cafeteria as far as I can tell," Oscar said, taking a bite of greasy pizza.

"Did you see that sweet dude with the spiky hair?" Brianne offered.

"Sweet?"

"Come on, Mom, I was just kidding."

"We saw him. He was staring at a Miss Slack, the girl in charge of the orientation. Why, do you think?"

"Either he thought she was pretty or they are buddies, if you know what I mean." Brianne grinned mischievously at them both. "Perhaps they have something to do with Roxanne's death."

"You can't be serious." Oscar rolled his eyes. "Just because they were staring at each other?"

Brianne shrugged and took a bite of her sub. It had wrinkly green lettuce protruding from the sides.

"Did you open the bun first and look inside?" Oscar asked.

"No." Brianne stopped chewing.

"I would if I were you. This place isn't called Greenfield Cafeteria for nothing."

Clues

Before leaving the cafeteria, Susan had managed to speak with a couple of the workers there, but no one knew anything more about the murder of Roxanne Anderson than she'd managed to retrieve once she'd returned home and read the article in the paper.

Roxanne Lee Anderson, or "Roxy" as her friends called her, was found dead at the yearly Halloween Bazaar held at Inglewood Fair Grounds in Walnut Hill this past Friday.

Anderson, a college student at Lowell, studied French and History, and was said to have been fond of friendships that went beyond her typical circle. According to Johnny Reimbolt, a fiery freshman from her class, Anderson preferred friends that stood apart from the average group.

"She was friends with everyone," said Reimbolt, "she even liked me," pointing to his hair, which had been gelled to stick up at every angle of his head. "She liked everyone and most things that had to do with architecture." He pointed to Rowan Halls where the girl had lived.

"I mean, these places are pretty old, but that's how she liked them."

Anderson's parents, Craig and May Anderson, residents of Walnut Hill, would not comment on their daughter's death other than to say she was "sweet and careful about everything. They loved and would miss her very much."

This is the second of two deaths that have occurred at the Halloween Bazaar, an event that has been running without a hitch for ten years, said Justine Commons, organizer of the event. "I could hardly believe it when I heard," she said. "The bazaar halted in that very moment. The next morning, everyone here with a booth was asked to clean up and go home."

"So, maybe we should speak with that Johnny kid," Brianne said, "and find out what happened at the *Halloween Bazaar* those ten years ago. What about the woman in charge of the thing?"

"We'll get to her last. Let's start with a bit of history. We'll go to the library first, see what we can find, and then head over to the campus."

With just a little searching, the details of that day emerged.

The death of Mable Savoy had occurred near the woman's restroom. She'd fallen, they'd soon discovered, and wore a pacemaker. They'd closed up shop out of respect for the woman, who'd had little to no family. A frequent visitor of the *Halloween Bazaar*, Mable Savoy had had more than her fair share of cats. Seemed she had always taken the strays in.

"Funny."

Susan restacked the newspapers. "Well, I guess that's that," she said. "A woman dies of a heart attack at the *Halloween Bazaar*. No murder here, just a tired old woman."

Returning the stack of newspapers to the front desk, the two made their way to the college.

***

"So, you're not cops?" Johnny asked, looking quizzically at Brianne.

"No, stupid."

"We're just interested in what happened to your friend," Susan said, hoping her daughter hadn't offended him.

"She was murdered. I can't believe anyone would stab her in the head."

"With a shoe," Brianne added.

"You heard that, too? It wasn't in the paper."

"I was there. Only one of the two shoes have been found — evidently."

"Evidently."

"Did you know her?" Brianne asked.

"Only vaguely, though she seemed to know everyone."

"But you knew where she lived and what she liked to do."

"Everyone knew that." He looked at Susan. "So, you're her mother. Hardly look like one."

"Thank you," Susan replied.

Brianne blushed.

"I mean, most moms have this terrifically bad hair style, and their clothes are from the 50s."

Susan tried hard not to stare. Today the boy's blonde hair spiked on one side only. He wore an orange shirt with purple pants.

"So, what else do you know about Roxanne?"

"Only that she was hard to get. I mean, I hardly knew her but somehow she knew everyone on a first name basis after only the first week of school."

"In the entire college?"

The boy blushed. "Duh. Probably not, but it seemed like that. How did you know her?"

"Spent a few minutes with her right before she was murdered."

"So, it was you, then?"

"Me, what?"

"You."

Brianne stomped her foot, a typical two-year-old thing to do, but just like her. "I didn't kill her, that's why I'm trying to find the killer!"

"You mean you and your mom."

"Well, yes. You are the most disgusting guy I've ever met."

He smiled. "You're pretty cute when you get mad. Just like Foxy Roxy —" He stopped mid-sentence. "I mean, she could have had any guy she wanted — almost."

"Except you."

"How did you guess?"

He walked away, across the grass to *McElderly*, leaving them gaping.

"So, what do you make of that?" Susan asked.

***

Fortunately, the conversation with Justine Commons went a bit smoother.

As they sat across from her desk at *True and Vine*, there was no mistaking the reason for her position in all things public relations. She not only had an eye for beauty (her office looked like the next fixed-up fixer-upper) her papers, few that they were, were neatly stacked to the left of the computer. A jar for pens sat to the right of her very clean desk, and the woman sat up straight in her chair as she spoke to them — obviously fully engaged in the question that had prompted the conversation. But that wasn't all. Everything was pink.

"Well, what can I tell you," she began, tapping her left index finger on her bottom lip. "You know I wasn't there."

Susan nodded.

"The police haven't said anything to me. I mean, all I know is that the woman was killed, right in the head, with a stiletto heel. Can you imagine that, right there in *Clothing to Die For*."

"*Clothing to Die For*?"

"Yes, didn't you notice? You said you were there. The place was called, *Clothing to Die For*. And I guess *she* did." The woman covered her mouth suddenly, but not before a slight smile had creased her lips. "Don't think me crass, it's just sort of funny that's all."

"Sort of," Susan mumbled.

"Well, she died there, right by the clothing, with no shoes on her feet, so says the owner who had been busily filling the racks when the murder occurred. The other one must have left with the murderer. You know we had to send them home. The police had to check things. And so, they checked, but they didn't tell me a word. What I know I found out from Cardigan. Funny, don't you think?"

"What?" Brianne asked, but Susan already knew. And it wasn't funny.

"The man, the owner, Fred. He sells clothes and his last name..."

Brianne blushed. "Oh," she said.

"Well, I couldn't believe it. It gave me the creeps. Can you imagine someone carrying off a black shoe as some kind of trophy? Someone was sure to see *that*."

"Did anyone?" Susan asked, her heart pumping within her chest.

"Fred didn't, and he stood right there. He was looking down, putting the shirts on the rack, filling up where holes had been, you know, when he heard a scream and looked up. There on the floor, just a few feet from him was the girl."

"Did you speak with anyone else that day?"

"You mean the vendors? Why, sure. No one had seen a thing, though those close by had gotten up from their chairs or whatever they were doing to take a look."

"Are you sure?" Susan shifted uneasily on her chair and looked behind the woman. On the back wall was a picture of a pelican. Pink. She suddenly realized that all of the accessories on the table, the cup holder, the stapler, the paperclip holder — everything was pink.

"As sure as I'm sitting here. Any other questions?"

"Can you take us to where the murder occurred?"

Justine shook her head. "I don't think so, at least not yet. The police still have the place yellow cautioned taped. I would be glad to take you there when things have been cleaned up, however."

"How soon will that be?" Susan asked.

"Probably within a day or two I expect, but you really don't think you'll find any clues there by then, when the police are finished, do you?"

"I never thought of that." Brianne looked over at her mother for some sort of support.

"Well, I guess that's it," Susan said, standing up. Brianne followed and together they walked to the closed door. "If you think of any other questions, please come on by, I love visitors."

The woman smiled and directed them out the door but not before she stopped them. "You know, come to think of it, you may want to talk to Carly, too – and Mark Rand. I don't know why I thought of him, he doesn't work regular hours here, just occasionally for big events."

"Oh. What about Carly?"

"She had the booth across the way from Fred's — called *Holiday Hours*. They were sort of hitting it off, if you know what I mean, and I have a sneaking suspicion that the two were engaged in conversation when the scream occurred. Now that I think of it, she told me something sort of strange, though at the time I didn't think anything of it."

Susan stood like molten rock as she waited. She wondered if either of them could hear the pounding of her heart. And then it came:

"Carly, her last name is Petersen, with an 'e' — she said that she'd heard a child crying before the scream. I can't believe I forgot that. Do you think it means anything? There was this little voice crying and she was about to find out who, when a loud, piercing scream stunned her into stopping where she was and not moving forward."

"A child's cry?" Susan asked. "In the same direction as the victim's?"
"That's what she told me."

***

"*Holiday Hours*. That's a cute name."

"I guess." Susan shrugged, more intent on getting home and running their discoveries past her husband over contemplating Carly's business name.

It was only five in the evening and Oscar was already pulling things out of the refrigerator.

"How was it?" he asked when he saw them.

"Good," Brianne offered, sitting down on a kitchen chair.

"Great!" echoed Susan. "Where's your dad?"

"Asleep in the chair as always. I think he needs another check-up, Mom. He sleeps more than he's awake."

Susan turned to the living room. Sure enough, Henry was asleep. Walking to him she tried to block out the sudden feeling of loneliness that filled her heart. She would always love Henry, even in this — this separation from her. Her son was right. He was always asleep, always groggy or frustrated or distant. Ever since the heart attack...

"Oh, Susan. You're back. Sorry. I was so tired."

"Brianne and I found out some things."

"That's great, but can I hear about them later? When will you be fixing dinner?"

"Soon. How are you doing?" She tried not to get angry because he appeared to want food more than any information from her, still, it was difficult pushing aside the thought.

***

"I told you! Stay out of my room!" Brianne was in an uproar. She stomped up the hall. "Oh Mom! It's happened again!" Her daughter's face burned hot, her lips quivering in frustration.

"What?"

"He... he's been in my room again."

"Who?"

"Oscar, of course!"

26

Oscar was a white-blue, as if he'd suddenly forgotten to take a breath. But maybe his perceived skin tone had more to do with the situation than anything else. "I told you. I didn't go in there! I didn't touch anything!"

Brianne turned, lifting her hands and shaking them in rage. "I told you, the next time you went into my room..."

"What? That you'd tell on me? Really, Brianne, how old are you anyway? And what was I supposed to have touched anyway?"

"As if you didn't know."

Fortunately, at least in Susan's eyes, arguing like this happened rarely in their household, but with a brother and sister living in practically the same space, it was only a matter of time when tempers would flair and the ceiling would rise.

"Stop!" Susan wasn't sure where her husband was; even during the racket she hadn't seen him. He hadn't even yelled from the bedroom or office — his two comfort spots as of late. Thanksgiving break was in full force for both of them, and Susan wasn't sure if she could outlive the last two days her children had at home before returning.

Brianne placed her hands on her hips and stared at her. "Well, what are you going to do, Mom? You'd better ground him — or something."

"I think..." Susan began, because the idea had suddenly called out to her that these two were no longer children. "I think you two need to work this out yourselves. You're old enough."

"Mom!"

"No Mom, me. I mean it. Go over to your brother and work this out."

"I don't want to sit in his stinky room." She stuck her tongue out at him.

"Then sit in the kitchen. Where's Dad?"

"The last time I saw him he was reading the newspaper."

"Good. I'll talk to Dad and you two can speak to one another — nicely — in the kitchen. Fair enough?"

Oscar smirked. "I have nothing to hide," he said.

"I know he did it," Brianne offered smugly, turning from them both and walking past her and into the kitchen. The chair made a slight squeaking sound and then it was silent.

"Sounds like she's ready for you."

"Thanks, Mom," her son offered, brushing past her.

27

Susan took a deep breath and followed Oscar, stopping in the living room to wake her sleeping

husband. The newspaper had fallen to the floor and his mop of red hair had traveled into his eyes.

Henry...

She sat next to him, taking his hand. "Henry?" she whispered.

He didn't stir.

"Henry?!"

His eyes blinked as he looked over at her. "What?"

"We need to talk."

He smiled at her slightly. "Are the children okay?"

So, he had heard.

"Yes, they're working things out in the kitchen."

"Good. So, what did you learn about yesterday?" he asked groggily, still holding her hand.

"Just that we need to speak with the owners of *Clothing to Die For...*"

"You mean that dive on Main? I can't believe they do any business. Walked through the place a couple of years ago, when you asked about a new purse and it was like stepping over tombstones. The place was a mess. More like a junk yard."

"Really?"

"So how did their booth look like at the event?"

"Not sure. I didn't notice it, though I did notice the other place to some degree."

"Wasn't that where the girl was murdered?"

"Yes, stiletto heel and all. What about the Christmas store?"

Henry released her hand and stood. He paced slowly in the living room, taking occasional peeks into the kitchen. The kids were pretty quiet.

"Evidently, this ah, Carly Petersen with *Holiday Hours* heard a child crying right before the scream, in the direction of the murder. At least that's what she told Justine Commons, the event coordinator at *True and Vine.*

"A child, not very interesting. How many children do you think frequent such a place with their mothers?" He grinned wickedly at her.

"Okay, okay... I thought the same thing, but it could mean something, couldn't it?"

***

When Monday arrived, so did the regular school hours. Just six months to go and Oscar would graduate. Of course, Brianne had some three years to go, but she could see it now, as if the day had already arrived. Her daughter was smart, almost too smart for her age, and yet the emotional tirades continued to amaze her. How like Brianne to suspect her brother of prying into her things, when it was obvious he worked hard at his studies, and had no time to snoop around.

And then there was the new girlfriend.

Yes, somehow, she'd actually become a hit, though Susan hadn't yet met her. Maybe his sister had thought he'd entered her room to swipe something for the girl... Who knew? She had tried to speak to Oscar after the visit but his mouth had been as closed as a can of beans.

"So, we can work out things ourselves, but you have to know what we said. Thanks, but no thanks, Mom. I love you, but you've got to trust me on this one." He'd smiled after that, and she'd followed suit. He was right, she supposed, and they appeared to be back to normal, so what was she worried about?

As she and Henry drove to *Holiday Hours*, she visited with him about the boy named Johnny. Though as tight lipped as her son had been this morning, he did seem a bit more than the average 'strange' when it came to a pre-adult. He'd known the victim, she recalled, about as much as everyone else. She had been popular, evidently, and something to remember with the guys. And she knew from the orientation that he had a thing for Miss Slack. Why was she thinking of her now? Probably because she'd forgotten to ask him about the girl he'd been staring at during orientation.

"Do you think the crime could have been a crime of passion?" she asked now as her husband pulled into a parking stall. "I mean, jealously is big at this age. Maybe Roxy was mixed up in something."

"Obviously," Henry answered, turning off the ignition, "or she wouldn't be dead."

***

Mr. Cardigan was older than Susan expected, and his clothing choices reflected a by-gone era. He almost reminded her of Mr. Rogers from that children's show on PBS. The man was of about the same build, too.

Still, as Susan looked around at the boxes piled in every corner, and the lack of space between aisles, there was something else that wasn't quite right about Fred Cardigan. She could smell it.

"I was really looking to make a profit at that event," he began after they'd introduced themselves. The man was wispy thin and shorter than normal for a man. Susan guessed about 5'7". "I have been hurting some this past year and was hoping I would be able to pull myself out of the proverbial red hole."

"Red..."

"Just a phrase of speech, sonny. Just a phrase. Business is tough. My father left me this shop and I've tried to get it out of the red, but you know how things are. Times are tough."

Henry nodded. She watched his sallow expression from the corner of her eye, trying not to stare. Though her husband stood straight and tall, it almost seemed as if the motion took great effort. She could almost see his wandering eyes trying to find a place to lie down.

"So, what did you see?"

"You mean that day?"

"We need to know every detail you can remember," Susan offered.

"I've already told the police. Ask them."

"We want to know from your own lips."

"She was beautiful, you know. But she would never have given me the time of day."

"Who?" Henry asked, though Susan was pretty sure she already knew.

"Carly Petersen, of course." He blushed awkwardly. "I'm just too different. Even ten years ago, I wouldn't have been any match for her."

"What can you tell us?"

Fred laughed and adjusted his blue cardigan. "She's pretty friendly. Almost too friendly if you know what I mean." He paused, taking them in.

"She was interested in you." Henry's words were shallow, almost like someone else was speaking them.

"Maybe," Fred continued, turning from them and walking around the messy counter. Piles of boxes and papers scattered the top, practically hiding the cash register. For the first time Susan wondered if they were the only customers in the store.

"We had a good talk, that is, until some child screamed bloody murder."

Susan's ears perked up.

"And the scream, did you see anything unusual before the scream?" Henry asked.

"No. But after the scream there was terrific movement within my booth."

"Where was Carly at the time?"

"Oh, pretty close to me, at the edge of her booth, yelling just a bit over the crowd — you know how that can be — and I was laughing at something she'd said. She'd told a joke. Oh, what was it? Anyway, before I could form an answer, everyone rushed behind me. And then, it was almost as if I knew. The girl was dead."

"How did you...?"

"Know? I'm not really sure. I'd seen her briefly as she'd entered my booth. But seconds later, my eyes were on Carly..." he blushed again. "It's strange, you know. Seeing the girl and then suddenly hearing a child scream and the crash of something behind me. Almost like hangers clanking, but not landing on the floor. It startled me."

The back of Susan's neck prickled.

"I turned from Carly and walked around two racks before I found her lying in her own blood."

A strange sensation felt its way up Susan's back. She couldn't explain it. But the words, well, they just didn't feel right.

Turning of the Key

Hope stood in the doorway. "So, what do you think I do with my time?" she asked.

"I'm sorry, Mother. I'm just worried about you."

"Why?"

"Are you going to let me in?"

"I don't know."

"I'm here to help you. The kids are at school and Henry is working."

"I can hardly believe that. How is he anyway?"

"Henry? Fine. Fine."

"Can't be all that fine if you're here at my place trying to weasel information out of me."

Hope's husband had been placed in jail and the final verdict surrendered — he would be in prison for life with a possibility of parole in ten years — his sentence was pretty heavy, seeing as he was also partially responsible for the poisonings poured out in the last mystery. Unfortunately, her mother had surrendered herself to the gloom.

"I'm not here to weasel out anything," she said through the door. "I just thought you might like some company."

The door opened a crack. "If there's one word about my husband..."

"Like I said."

The door opened and Susan was ushered in. "Sit in your regular spot," her mother said, directing her to the white sofa.

Susan didn't have a moment to lose. Before the door shut, smack dab in front of her face, she walked briskly to the sofa and sat down. Blinking over at her mother, she sat in a chair across the way — in the same chair that

William had sat in himself the last time she'd seen him in this room. But her mother — she looked pale and old.

"How are you feeling?" Susan began, trying to calm her pattering heart. Why was it like this anyway? Why did she feel as if she was talking to a stranger, sitting at a job interview, fishing for words that weren't really in her heart?

"Fine. You?"

She wanted to ask her mother if she missed William even though she despised everything about him. She wanted to ask her if she cried at night missing him, or threw things at the picture she had hanging in the bedroom of them together — if it was still there.

"I'm good. The kids are growing. Oscar is considering Lowell."

"That rink-e-dink school?"

"For your information, Lowell is a fine school."

"Not after that girl was murdered there," her mother offered.

"She wasn't murdered at the college. It was at that..."

"Oh yes, the craft show. How could I forget? A miracle you didn't get killed." She rolled her eyes and crossed her legs. "Really, Susan, you do get around, don't you?"

She must have paled. "How come you hate me?" she asked.

Her mother reached for a glass of something that she'd poured before her visit. It was in a sparkling clear wine glass. The liquid was red. She took a sip. "I suppose you would like some," she asked, though not with a question. "I don't hate you, Susan. I do hate the choices you make, however."

Unlike yours? Susan thought but didn't say.

"I love Henry. And you can't blame me for that. He loves me, unlike my first husband who just wanted to control my entire life."

"I liked Bob. Sure, he wasn't as fond of you at first... but I can be pretty persuasive when I want to be."

"You mean like now?" Susan stood and brushed past her, trying to keep her legs steady, her eyes straight ahead. Why had she come? Why? She reached for the door knob.

"Susan?"

She turned. Her mother suddenly faced her. In the olden days, when she was young and free and believed everything her mother said or did, she'd believed her mother had loved her. But now?

"I'm sorry."

Susan blinked.

"Really." Placing the glass on the side table her mother reached for her. "I'm just worried about my William. After all he has done I still love him. Can you understand that?"

Susan nodded, though she wasn't sure why. After all that Bob had done to her, she cared for him even less, though she did feel sorry for him. How could her mother love a man that had almost murdered her friend?

"I may love William for a long time. It may take years for me to get past this one. I need you to be patient with me. Can you do that?"

Susan smiled, but she wondered, in that moment when her mother really needed a genuine answer, if she would be able to give it. Even worse, her questions would just have to wait for another day.

***

"Honey, is that you?"

Susan placed her purse on the table and went in the direction of Henry's make-shift detective agency. It was just a corner of the bedroom for now, and there were papers stacked on either side of the computer. He turned to watch her come in.

Henry looked better today. His color was even, and his face pinker than she'd seen it in weeks. "I can't believe it!" he said, forcing a piece of paper in her direction. "And you won't believe it either."

"What?"

"I've got the case. The one you're working on."

"No."

"Everything's here."

She looked down at the piece of paper. Roxy's parents?"

"Yep."

"The letter came today while you were out with your mother. So, how was lunch?"

"Lunch? Oh, we didn't get to that." She knew it sounded like something you'd check off a long list, but it was sort of like that with her mother.

"What did you get to?"

She looked down again at the letter:

Dear Mr. James,

You don't know me but you're probably aware of my daughter and her death...

"Well?"

"Sorry. Can I read the letter first?"

Henry blanched. "What? Oh, yes."

I know that my daughter was murdered, and I believe (we believe) we have a pretty good idea of who took her life. Enclosed you will find Roxanne's obituary and a token of our seriousness in this matter.

Susan looked up. Henry was holding up a check.

"How much?"

"A five-hundred-dollar deposit. Now, before you say anything, I think I'm going to take this one on."

"Why?"

She wasn't sure, but Susan suddenly felt that something was terribly wrong. How did the woman know that Henry was a detective anyway? How had they gotten their address? He wasn't in the phone book — no one put their information there anymore anyway — and he hadn't yet finished the website with his credentials.

"I don't get it. Here I am, trying to figure out who killed the girl, and they ask you."

"Don't be jealous, Honey." He stood, placing the check on his messy desk. "We can work on it together."

Susan wasn't so sure. She peered down once more and finished the letter:

We can be reached at 555-985-3284 at your earliest convenience.

Sincerely,

May and Craig Anderson

"How do you think they got your information?" Susan asked.

"Maybe you said something. You've been there, right?"

"No. I would have told you if I had."

Her husband raised an eyebrow.

"Okay, I *might* have told you. The truth is I haven't had a chance to visit Roxanne's parents yet."

"Well, now we can visit together. Want to call, or should I?"

***

Brianne and Oscar were busy at school two days later when she and Henry were finally able to travel to Walnut Hill for a visit. The Anderson place was near *Honesty House*, but not close enough to resemble the buildings Susan was most used to. Evidently, a new development had begun, and the large homes that they drove by on this particular November night were something to write home about.

"What do you think they'll be like?" Susan asked as they pulled into the steep driveway. A large curved lamppost greeted them, as well as a 3-car garage.

"Oh, I don't know. Maybe they'll be nice."

He turned off the ignition and opened his door. Susan reached for her door and followed him up the front steps. "That's right, Thanksgiving is coming up," he said easily, winking at her sideways. "The door is pretty festive."

The door opened. A young boy with dark hair looked out. "You must be the detectives," he said.

"Yes, we are," Henry said, smiling. "And you are?"

"Kent."

"Hi, Kent. Can we come in?"

"Let them in, Kenny..."

Susan patted the boy's head as they walked past him. A teenager who looked about the same age as her deceased sister, her long dark hair almost dripping into the cup of milk before her, held a graham cracker. "Mom says to come in here." She pointed with the cracker to the living room at the right of the kitchen. "They'll be down in a second."

Henry took her hand. "Thank you," he said, as they walked past the girl who had a striking resemblance to her dead sister.

The room was nicely furnished in cream and blue, with just a hint of yellow. They sat on a cream couch with blue and white pillows and waited. Fortunately, they didn't have to wait long.

In moments Mr. and Mrs. Anderson were traveling down the short steps to the living room. They took a place across from them closest to the window. Mrs. Anderson spoke first.

"I'm so glad you could make it," she said, looking more at Henry than herself. "Things have been in an uproar over here, as you can imagine, but no matter. It's time for our girl to get what she deserves."

Craig nodded and reached for his wife's hand. "Roxy was going far, and her time here was cut much too short. If only she'd listened to us about that Reimbolt character."

"You mean the boy at the college?" Henry asked.

"Surprisingly, yes." May reached a narrow hand through her stunning black hair. "You've got to understand. When you send your children to college, you hope they will choose good friends. We never knew Johnny, at least not directly, but we knew plenty about him. Our daughter, Katrine, is Roxy's twin."

Susan looked up and into the kitchen. Katrine was still dipping her crackers into the milk and eating them. She didn't turn.

"She attended the same college?"

"Yes... and no. Actually, Katrine was gung-ho on the idea in the beginning," Craig said, looking up at his daughter for only an instant before meeting Susan's eyes again. "Only, she dropped out last semester — we had to…"

"Not hard, Dad. Boring."

"So, what did you study?" Susan asked, loudly enough for the girl to hear though she'd obviously heard fine even when the volume of voices was turned down.

The girl turned. "Math mostly. I wanted to study Interior Design but Mom and Pops wouldn't have that."

"So, what are you doing now?" Susan asked.

"Work up the street; grocery." She turned back to her treat and dipped a full cracker into the milk.

"Children are different, you know. You have children?" Craig asked.

Henry nodded. "Two."

"Then you know how different they can be."

"I heard that," Katrine returned from the other room.

"So, what about this Johnny Reimbolt," Susan asked. "Why was he such a bad character?"

A sudden push of a chair signaled that Katrine had left her spot. She was heading to the sink. With another plunk the dishes were deposited. "That kid was no good, but Roxy liked him, just like she liked everyone — the creeps included." Katrine stopped near the stairs.

"Want me in there?" she asked. "I can tell you all sorts of stories my parents have no idea about."

"Like what?" Susan asked.

"Well..." she blinked her green eyes mischievously, "about guys of course. Roxy was into guys. She could talk to them about anything."

Susan was curious about the word, *anything*, but decided to remain silent.

"You can sit if you promise to stay focused," said her father, brushing his thick hands against his jeans. "And you've got to promise."

Katrine blinked and bounded into the room. "I guess you could call me the loser child," she said, sitting down at the other end of the couch.

"Katy..."

"Okay, Dad."

"We're concerned that this boy, Johnny, is nothing but trouble. He's still in college and we're worried that he might attack some other girl," May said.

"You mean like Matty?"

"Who?" Henry asked.

"Matilda Slack, but of course she doesn't go by that name, who would?" Crossing her legs, Katrine stared at Henry for a full minute before she had occasion to look her way, and by then the silence was deafening.

"So, Johnny made friends with our girl when she first arrived," Craig began. "Friendly as she is, Katrine was worried so she'd call us and let us know how close the two were becoming."

"I can speak for myself. I only called them twice. The first time, Roxy was going out on a date with him. The second time she was crying because he said he wanted to break up. He liked some other girl."

"What other girl?" Henry asked.

"Matty. Everyone hates her. She thinks she is better than everyone. Can you imagine in college, doing some sort of high school spin off? But that's how she is — how she was with Roxy. They never got along."

"How do you know?" asked Susan.

"Duh, it was evident. To her face my sister was all nice and cuddly, talking to her like she was one of her hundred other friends, even speaking to her nicely after Johnny broke up with her and turned his attention on Matty, but I knew the truth."

"What truth?" Susan asked.

"She hated her, and would have killed her if she'd gotten the chance. Only Matty beat her to it."

"Katy!" her father shouted. "If you can't —"

"Okay, Pops. Just a little slip up." She smiled. "I'm fine now." Katrine adjusted her hair by taking the elastic from around her wrist and creating a pony tail.

Susan and Henry turned to the parents.

"We apologize for our daughter's outbursts. She knows better."

"I'm going to be out of here soon enough, when I've saved enough money," Katrine said, tightening the elastic. "I will be out of here for — good."

The static in the air was electric. Susan wondered how these three ever got along, and how the boy, Kent, fit into the family dynamics. Was he quiet and shy or loud and obnoxious like his older sister? Only time would tell. For now, he wasn't in the room and probably wouldn't be invited to take part in such a discussion. Frankly, Susan somehow wished she could slide under the carpet herself. But they needed answers and knowing something more about Johnny and his girlfriend, Matty could be the ticket they all needed to find the killer.

***

"I can't believe it. It's like going to my mother's house!"

Henry smiled at the joke, though it did hold some truth, at least for Susan. They'd spent roughly two hours at the Anderson home, and had a slew of information on Johnny Reimbolt and Matty Slack, the blonde-haired girl who'd been in charge of the orientation meeting they'd attended. What they didn't know was why the boy, Johnny, had said nothing about being Roxy's boyfriend, why he'd in fact lied about their connection.

"What do you think Johnny is hiding?" Henry asked. He pulled out of the driveway and they made their way home, though there was really no need. The kids were grown and could fend for themselves. Still, it had always comforted Susan to know that the house wasn't empty when her children returned.

It was cold out and plenty icy, but they had new tires on the older vehicle, and Henry was a pretty expert driver no matter the weather. He turned to her briefly.

"There's a reason he didn't tell us about his involvement with Roxanne. I think we'd better talk to him again. I also wonder about that Matty Slack. Did you get a chance to talk to her?"

"Not yet. She's a hard one to find."

"Can't be too hard. You found Johnny."

"She's gone."

"From the college? When did you find that out?"

"Made a few calls. Quite a few people at the school wouldn't give her name out — and then I hit the jackpot. An intern..."

"That would do it." Henry smiled.

Returning up the drive, they were just in time to see Oscar and Brianne going inside. "What do you think? Should I enlist the help of Brianne?" Susan asked. "She may be able to get something from Johnny that we can't."

"About that." Henry pulled the keys from the ignition. "I... think you should let her try. I'm pretty tired. I don't know what it is, but I can't seem to get the adrenaline pumping like I used to."

She removed her seat belt and touched him on the shoulder. "Henry I —"

"Now, I don't want you to worry about me, the doctor said I should take it easy, and maybe I should listen."

Susan opened her mouth to speak and then shut it.

Hot Pursuit

The first of December arrived, and along with it even more snow and even colder temperatures. Still, she and her family were trying to decide how to make the best use of the weather.

"Let's go snowboarding," Oscar said first, as if they had mountains for doing such a thing in the first place.

"Fly kites!" Brianne interjected, smiling over at him and winking.

"Kites!?"

"Just kidding. But it's more realistic than going snowboarding!"

"Not to mention we don't own any of the equipment," said Henry.

Susan smiled. "What about a picnic? We used to do that all of the time."

"Yeah. Remember the time in front of *Honesty House* when Brianne said she wanted to be a detective? We don't have to eat out but we can visit over there. I sort of miss that place."

"How is Jane anyway?" Brianne asked.

Susan's thoughts tumbled. Actually, it had been weeks since she'd even checked in. She'd seen her friend once or twice following the murder, but after that, things had just kept piling up.

"I thought you were friends," Oscar said.

"Well, yes. We are."

"Then I have the best idea — ever! Let's surprise your friend and take her a picnic!" Brianne squealed.

"You'd really want to do that?"

Henry smiled. "Why not?"

"How about you?" Susan turned to Oscar. He smiled.

"Sure. Will we have chicken?"

***

As it turned out, having a picnic on the last day of November was the perfect choice. Jane Dove, Susan's once upon assistant at *Honesty House* now turned owner, had already gathered the children inside when they'd decide to drop in for a visit — chicken in hand.

"I was missing you something terrible!" she began. "How is the murder investigation going?"

"Fine," Henry began, handing her the first chicken leg.

"We're sort of working on it together," added Brianne, momentarily gazing over at Oscar who had dipped his fingers into the basket, withdrawing two pieces, a breast and wing.

"Don't go for that sort of thing," Oscar relayed after the first chew. "I mean, what do we care that some girl was murdered? She wasn't even related."

The comment sounded callous and unfeeling, but Susan decided to let it go. One day, perhaps even sooner than Oscar realized, he would be in love — maybe even with that girl he was always taking out that they'd never met.

Still, the thought continued to whirl in her head later when she and Henry sat together in the living room talking. She'd lost a sister to a murder as well as an ex-husband. And even when a loved one hadn't been in the picture, she'd still been willing to search for the killer until he was found.

So, what was it about her anyway? Why care about a college girl she didn't even know?

Jane had been so happy to see them and the visit had been justified, but in the end, Susan had returned to her thoughts of detective work and had worried about her son's comment. What did it mean after all? Why couldn't she be satisfied with her husband and children? Without *Honesty House* in the forefront, her life was somewhat empty, she knew that, so maybe just maybe she sleuthed because she had some holes in her life to cover up. What else could it be?

At times, she'd felt like a death magnet. Not only with her seeming attraction to murders, but because of her husband's ongoing health condition. Oh, what would her husband think about that? He sat next to her. How long did her husband have? Would she find him the next day — dead — because of his heart condition? Would his life be over easy, just because of his day to day interactions with her? But of course, she was being silly. She wasn't a death magnet just as she wasn't a real detective.

Still, she worried. How much longer did she have with him?

Thoughts continued to stir within her, thoughts that wouldn't be silenced.

***

"Leave me alone!" Johnny ran from them, his white shoes pounding the snow outside the front office where they had first spotted him.

Susan raced at his heals, shouting back: "Why did you lie about Roxy?"

"I didn't!"

She huffed at his side as she tried to keep up. "You did! I talked with her parents and her sister!"

"Her sister?" He stopped, holding his chest. "Why do you care anyway?"

Susan breathed in and out heavily. Henry wasn't with them.

"Wait. Here." She stopped Johnny with her hand and raced back.

"Are you alright?"

Henry was pale. He was holding his chest. "What do you think?" he asked.

"I'm sorry, I just —"

"You just lost... Johnny..."

Susan turned. The boy was almost out of sight.

"Don't run, I'll get him!" she yelled. Turning the corner, she didn't see him, though he revealed himself a moment later. He was getting into a red car — just barely — maybe she could still catch him.

Their own car was just a few rows down. Maybe she'd reach it in time and follow him out. She had to try. Increasing her speed — her own shoes digging into the snow as she raced to catch up with him — she watched as the boy jumped into his car and sped south from the parking lot.

In only moments, she was in her own car, racing behind him. Though not seeing him directly, she worked her way around the buildings until she'd reached the main road. There he was, just now turning onto a connecting road.

"You won't get away from me!" she screeched, pushing on the gas and paying little attention to the speed bumps and stops signs as she clambered passed. Turning the corner, she saw him again, but he was too far ahead for her to track him until she'd again rounded the corner.

He was entering a shopping mall.

Two cars were ahead of her now, and they were driving slower than molasses. "Get out of my way!" she screamed again, blocked by their inconsiderateness. The light turned green and she was off again. Turning the last corner she'd seen the red car enter, she followed the road until she reached the mall. Surveying the parking lot, she finally stopped the car and jumped out.

Where was he?

Getting back in the car she took the mall roads, slower this time, checking every stall, every passerby, hoping to see him. She tried for another half hour before she remembered that she'd left Henry at the college.

Running a hand through her hair, and brushing the sweat that had accumulated there, she took a deep breath and drove back to the college. Henry was standing near a curb waiting for her.

"I can't believe you did that, but I'm glad you did, sort of," he began. "Are you alright?"

For the first time Susan realized her heart was beating rapidly and her fingers were shaking. "I'm so sorry I left you!" she said.

"I'm just glad you didn't get into a car wreck," he answered.

"The car is fine! But Johnny..."

"I figured as much." He smiled again and reached for her, taking her into a long embrace. "I'm just glad you're okay."

Susan breathed in the smell of sweat. She laughed. "I'm a dope," she said, without meaning to. "A stupid dope."

He looked into her eyes. "No, you're not. You're just a wild detective!"

"Do you really think so?" she mumbled into his lengthening red hair. "I'm such a dunce."

"A beautiful dunce." Tears creased his eyes. "I haven't told you lately that I love you."

She returned the smile, and found his hair, brushing her fingers through it. "You fish," she answered.

Double Dunce

"Mom, you've got to be kidding!" Brianne stood in the hallway, her favorite place for arguments.

"I'm not kidding. Your father and I won't be working on this case so much. He... has things to do."

"What things?"

"His new business for one."

"But I thought the Anderson's were on his list. Didn't you say they were paying him?"

"Yes, but he needs some help. We'll do most of the leg work, and leave old Dad to do the paperwork. How does that sound?"

Brianne looked her over quizzically. "What's wrong with Dad?"

"He's just been working too hard lately..."

Brianne rolled her green eyes. "Really, Mom, I'm not that stupid. Is his heart bothering him again?"

"Sort of."

"Why won't you just tell me? Gads! You know I love detective work, but you've got to be pretty desperate to bring me in for real unless something terrible is going on." She paused, planting her hands in her back pockets. "Is it?"

Susan wondered how she'd be able to smooth over this piece of cake. Brianne wasn't little anymore; maybe she could deal with the truth. She was just about to explain herself when Brianne colored.

"Gads, Mom, I like to be with you, and I love to search things out. I would love to be a detective like Dad... and you, of course..."

Susan smiled. There it was again; the truth, at least the truth as everyone else seemed to think of it. "And you don't mind not spending time with your friends?"

"What friends? They think I'm a geek anyway."

"They do?" She looked deeply into her daughter's eyes. "Why?"

"I can't believe you haven't figured it out yet."

"Figured *what* out?"

"Okay, I like homework, okay? Oscar isn't the only kleptomaniac."

A sudden thought came to Susan's mind, one that had been swimming there ever since she and her husband's return from the Anderson's. How *had* they gotten his name and address?

"I'm sure I could help," Brianne breathed. "I mean, I know a lot about naming things."

"What?"

"I've already named my children, for one. And when I was a kid, before you took me on, you know, adopted me, I named every stuffed animal I owned, which wasn't much, but I named them."

...When she mentioned this conversation to Henry, he only laughed. Henry was at his desk, tapping his left leg, hoping she'd get the hint. She sat. "The Anderson's just called. They clued me in on a few other things."

"Like why they knew to call you in the first place?"

Henry blushed. "You thought about that, too, huh? They apologized again for their daughter's behavior and mentioned they were thankful their daughter, Roxanne, had felt to mention my name as a possible option. Evidently, the girl was worried about someone following her. She knew I used to work with the police and that you helped a bit on the side."

He stroked her hair. "Want to go out with me to lunch? I've been aching for some pizza."

"Sure. Is that all you're aching for?"

He grinned at her. "Probably not, but we'll have to take care of that later."

***

"I think I can make it," Henry said, taking her hand. "You can get Brianne's help the next time."

46

It was 11:30 a.m. and her children were still asleep, having watched a movie late into the evening. Susan watched her husband's eyes, and tried to get a clue as to how he was really feeling, but in the end, she'd relented. In pain or not, he seemed ready to go.

With a note left for Brianne and Oscar, they traveled to *True and Vine.*

Justine was finally able to take them through the Halloween bazaar; though, with everything finally cleaned up and the floors swept, there hadn't been much to see — until Justine had spoken about the dried blood that was still staining the cement floor.

"See it here?" she'd begun, pointing her finger at the slight trail that led away from the spot *Clothing to Die For* had been situated. Susan tried to remember the setup and Carly Petersen's booth across the way. "The drops stop here at the end of where *Holiday Hours* was located," she said, continuing to point down. "I wish there were more."

"As I remember, Roxy Anderson was found nearer the exit door."

"That's right."

They walked closer to the door. "I don't see anything," Henry said.

"Perhaps the girl was bleeding before she reached the area where she died," Susan said.

"But wouldn't drops of blood be nearer the door, too? It just doesn't make sense." Susan paced the area again.

"The police searched this area over and over and never found anything," Justine said.

"She was obviously bleeding before getting to the door. Maybe she was holding her head after that, stumbling to the door where she finally collapsed," Henry offered.

"Maybe. But what about where she'd fallen? There would have been blood there."

"Unless she fell on something that was removed before the police arrived."

Susan looked directly at Henry. "Why would someone do that?"

"I have no idea."

Justine was suddenly looking at them strangely. "I don't know if this means anything or not," she began, hands on her hips, her eyes scanning the room, "but later that day, after the police left, one of the cleaning ladies, a Mrs. Chartreuse, complained to me that she'd found blood on the floor by the paper towel dispenser. She thought it was - you know... it was in the bathroom and all, but she had a difficult time getting it up off of the floor."

"Sodium peroxide," Henry suggested.

"Yes, though the spot was somehow missed here, as you can see."

"Can we take a quick trip to the bathroom in question?" Henry asked, and Justine had led the way. But they hadn't found anything out of the ordinary, only a clean spot where the blood had been scrubbed clean.

Unresolved Questions

Henry sat up from bed. "Susan, Susan!" he yelled.

It was pitch dark, and no wonder, the clock read 3 a.m.

"What?" she mumbled into the darkness. She'd finally managed some sleep after some wicked dreams of blood drying in various places throughout her house. Had Oscar done it, or Brianne?

"Look! If that woman cleaned the floor in the lady's room, maybe she saw something else that she didn't relay to her boss."

Susan wiped at her eyes. "Really? Like what?"

"Okay, let's suppose the murder didn't happen at *Clothing to Die For*. We already know that blood was found further from the door than one might expect for someone dying right inside the booth. So, what if Roxy was stabbed with the stiletto in the lady's room? What if the killer did the deed — there?"

"Well, that would make more sense than the killer stabbing her right there in the booth. No one seemed to have seen anything, and why would they if the girl had somehow made it to the booth only to collapse there with the shoe."

"Only one shoe," Henry began, but Susan's head was already soaring. "What if Roxy was killed in the bathroom, and she managed to block her wound with some paper towels? Maybe she tried to stop the bleeding, and when that didn't work, she stumbled to get help."

Susan wiped her eyes again and faced Henry in the darkness. She could see him now, his red hair mussed, his breath smelling like dried onions. "But maybe she was in shock. Maybe she didn't realize how badly she'd been hurt. I've heard of folks getting stabbed and going into shock. They don't even know they've been stabbed until someone tells them so. She wonders why she's in the bathroom, why there is blood on her hands, wonders where her shoe has gone, leaves the bathroom, and stumbles to the booth where she dies."

"But why, *that* booth?" Henry asked.

Susan wasn't sure, but the girl must have been meeting someone.

"And who might have managed to kill her, even in the bathroom? Consider, Susan. With all of the people at the show, there had to be a lineup inside the restroom, there always is at these large events."

"Unless there wasn't. Really Henry, women don't spend hours in the bathroom as you might think. Maybe the killer was waiting for just the right time, when the bathroom was clear of other people, to make her move."

"So, it's a woman, huh?"

"How could a man get in a woman's bathroom without being noticed?"

"I can think of a few ways," answered Henry, smiling. "I mean, maybe the killer was a cross dresser."

"You've got to be kidding."

"I'm not. We've got to look at all of the options, right? Only then will we finally figure this mystery out."

***

Mrs. Chartreuse was younger than Susan expected. In her mind, the woman should have been in her mid-40s, but she was anything but that.

"Just call me Sadie," the young woman began, wiping her toilet wet hands against her white apron.

"You're married?" She shouldn't have asked, but Sadie was spectacular as well as curious. She wore her blonde hair in a ponytail, and her blue eyes were the color of the seashore. Her nails were cut short, befitting someone who cleaned for a living, but Susan was sure of one thing. The girl would have grown them longer if she could.

"Just a month ago, now. I can hardly believe it myself."

Henry was gaping. She nudged him.

"Yes, well, we have a few questions to ask you," he said.

She walked them out the restroom door. "There are chairs over there." She pointed up the hall and walked ahead of them. Brianne was with them, though she was silent. Susan wondered what she was thinking.

50

The folding chairs were pulled open. Everyone sat.

"Hi!" Brianne said at last, and Sadie smiled.

"Hi, yourself. You are related to these two, are you?"

"Unfortunately," she laughed. "I mean, yes they're my parents."

Susan's heart was pounding. This was good. Brianne was relaxing her. She was glad they'd brought her along. Henry was looking pale again, and she wondered if he was feeling ill as usual or only ill because Sadie sat next to him. She was being stupid, of course, but the young woman was beyond beautiful.

"Shoot."

Susan jumped.

"I mean, you can start now."

"Right. Justine Commons says you were the one who cleaned up the blood stain in the bathroom that day."

"That's correct. Actually, I was surprised the police didn't figure that part out. I mean, they're the police after all. But then again, I didn't say a word about it because they didn't ask me. Of course, Justine knew about it, she was the one who taught me what to use to get it clean. Did you know she came to me angry because I missed a spot?"

"Missed a spot, where?" Henry asked.

"In the main room where the vendors were. It's gone now, but I couldn't believe it. What was I supposed to do, check for more blood through the entire building?"

"Did you find any other blood other than the spot in the bathroom and the place where the girl died?" Susan asked.

"People can be so gross. You wouldn't believe what I find, what I have to clean up. Just last week, there was toilet paper and other stuff all over the floor by this one toilet. And the seat, well, someone had forgotten to wipe or something."

Brianne blushed. "Gads," she said, looking Sadie directly in the eyes. "That's why all the paper was on the floor."

"You got it."

Susan tried to smile. "No blood though?"

"Well, sometimes I find blood, you know... but not by the paper towel dispenser. People are washing their hands and stuff, and I guess they could have a cut, but that was the first time I'd seen a small puddle..."

"Did you find anything else?"

"No." Sadie stared at her. "I mean, there was blood, and the dispenser was empty. I can always expect most of the paper towels to be gone at the end of a big event, but not everything. The trash can wasn't even that full."

"So where do you think all the paper towels went?" Brianne asked.

"I figured whoever was bleeding had cleaned me out. When that woman was found dead, I thought it was pretty strange that she had a puncture in her head but nothing to hold the blood in with except for her hand. Still, I heard there was blood on it."

"You didn't see her then."

"No, but I know enough about cuts to know that you can only hold blood in for a short time before it goes spilling everywhere. We cleaned up after everyone had gone home and there were no bloody paper towels anywhere. Strange, don't you think?"

Brianne nodded. "Who else worked with you that night?

"Oh, I don't know. Let's see. There was Mark – here for a special assignment – and Cecil and little miss sunshine, Veronica Edwards." Sadie smirked. "I can't believe she's still working here."

"Why?" Henry asked.

"Always upset. About everything. She came in after me and told me off. Said in no uncertain terms that I was doing it all wrong, and that my cleaning would leave a mark and that everyone would know what I'd done."

"What *you'd* done?"

"As if I'd killed the girl myself. Can you believe it?"

***

"Gads, that girl gave me the willies," Brianne said.

Oscar was driving. He wasn't speaking. Susan understood the hesitation. Brianne was a natural, as natural and free as the skies were blue. Why, she'd questioned that woman like a pro.

"I wonder if she did it."

"The cleaning lady?" Susan asked.

"Yeah, she was weird, don't you think? She should have been a model or something, not stuck in some dead-end job with no future."

Henry laughed. "Where did you hear that?"

"What?"

"About dead-end jobs and no future?"

Brianne shrugged. "I don't know. So, what do you think? Could Sadie be the killer?"

Now it was Susan's turn to laugh, but her daughter's words did make her think.

***

"What motive would a girl like Sadie have over someone like Roxanne?"

"Well, they are both beautiful — "

Susan withdrew the bedspread. "I'm serious. What kind of motive would Sadie have over Roxanne?"

"Well, they seem to be about the same age. Why didn't you ask?"

"Why didn't you ask?" She slid into bed.

"I was more concerned learning about this Veronica Edwards. If she was with Sadie the night that Roxanne was murdered, then she might be the next person to speak with. Angry people do lots of things not conducive to friendliness."

"What?"

Henry slid into bed. "Made you listen."

She punched him in the arm. "I always listen."

"What about kissing, do you do that?" He pursed his lips, leaning in her direction.

"I'm serious." She bundled the blanket underneath her chin.

"So am I."

***

The cleaning lady, Veronica Edwards, was nothing to write home about. She was no surprise, not even in the same arena as Sadie Chartreuse. But she was friendly. Her large waist barely fit the white apron she wore. Her hair was slicked back. Though long, it was bound into an incredibly tight ponytail - the graying layers playing against her chubby face. She was short with thick ankles. But her smile was sweet and forthcoming.

"Oh, that dear girl. I can hardly believe it. When I found out I was beside myself."

"I know just what you mean." Brianne smiled her own sweet smile that appeared a bit forced to Susan. But she stood back and let the woman talk. Henry wasn't with them today, had complained of body aches, and so she and her daughter had come over together. Veronica was just clocking in when they walked through the front doors.

"I worked the night it happened, but I didn't see anything."

"Mrs. Chartreuse says..."

"I hoped you weren't going to start with her." The woman blinked at them, and her once calm face turned into a scowl. "I hate that girl. She is always hovering, always telling me what to do. I could be her mother, her mother!" She grabbed the cart on wheels leaning against the wall and pulled it towards her. "Don't believe anything she says."

"Why not?" Brianne asked, following closely behind her. Susan walked behind her daughter, hoping against all hope that Brianne wouldn't make the woman too angry.

"You're young. Younger than she is. How would you understand?" Veronica walked briskly in front of them now, hurling the cart to the left as she headed to the restrooms.

"I might —" Susan began. But the woman had quickly stopped and turned her large head at them.

"So, you're the mother." Her voice had calmed some, but her face was still red.

"Yes."

"Well, let me tell you something, it takes more than a pretty smile and winning ways to get me talking I can tell you that."

"We just want to know what you know about that day."

"I was cleaning. Just cleaning. Men's room. Same stuff. Pee on the floor. Paper towels everywhere. Men getting mad at me because I have to put the yellow sign out." She pointed to the sign. It read, 'Please wait. Cleaning in process.'

"Of course, the men don't get near as angry as the women do. That's why Ms. Chartreuse has me focus on the men's rooms. Get my drift?"

Susan couldn't figure out if the woman meant the comment figuratively or literally, but decided to play dumb. Brianne was silent, looking off into the distance, her lip trembling slightly.

"Did you see any paper towels with blood on them?"

"No."

"Anything strange?"

"You mean, stranger than what I've just told you."

Susan nodded.

Veronica smiled. "Sorry," she began, turning to her cart once more and heading to the men's room. "Feel free to take a look."

She knocked. "Cleaning service!" Veronica called, and when no one stepped up to open the door, they followed her inside. The place was empty.

"You're in luck. The men don't often frequent the place during the day unless there's a big event going on like a fishing or hunting show. Then it's all about scraping the floors and plugging your nose at the same time. It's a real feat I can tell you."

"Sounds like it," Susan said, opening the stalls and peering inside.

"Like I said, you're welcome to look."

Brianne peered down at the urinal, and Susan took a quick look at the sink as Veronica cleaned around it. "Sure beats me why someone would want to kill a girl like that. Beats me."

"Maybe someone was mad at her?" Brianne prompted, suddenly appearing to find her voice.

"Enough to kill? Probably not, though I have heard of people killing in a fit of anger. But that's usually relatives."

A sudden, eerie thought suddenly struck Susan. Parents like Mr. and Mrs. Anderson surely wouldn't kill their own daughter and then pay someone to find the killer, would they? But what about a twin sister?

"I heard that the deceased swiped tons of paper towels from the girl's restroom, towels we couldn't find afterwards. That's pretty strange to me. Have you checked with the person in charge of *Clothing to Die For*? It's almost as if the girl was sending a message."

Susan's heart stopped.

"A message?" she asked.

"Yeah. Don't you see it? She was murdered and walked over to that place clear from the bathroom before collapsing. It's at least a three-minute walk. Why not die in the lady's room, for Pete's sake?"

"We thought of that," Brianne mumbled.

"Smarty pants. They come in all shapes and colors."

"Gads, lady!"

The woman grinned. "Well, well, thank you very much. Now, you can see I'm busy." Veronica turned to the stall with a toilet brush in one hand and cleaner in the other.

"One more question?" Susan asked.

Veronica bent closer to the bowl and swished some pink cleaner around.

"Did Sadie, ah Mrs. Chartreuse say anything about the blood she found in the women's bathroom?"

"Sure."

Brianne blinked over at her, her face suddenly pale.

"She told me that there was a pool of blood about the size of an apple in there and that she would need some help cleaning it up. Only I was too busy to help her. And besides, she didn't really want me to be in there so I went back to my work. Anything else?"

"Well, if you don't mind."

A thought had suddenly formed itself in Susan's brain, and she just had to speak it. "The other blood, near *Clothing to Die F*or, did you see it?"

"Sure, I saw it, but it was just a spot."

"And where were you at the time of the murder?"

"You said one more question." The woman's complexion heated up.

"I know. Were you cleaning the men's restroom at the time?"

"No."

"Where were you?"

"There. At the spot."

"At the spot?"

"Yeah. Where the blood was. I looked down. After the scream, I looked down. There it was. Everyone rushed around me as if I wasn't there. I almost got trampled, but I didn't move. I just kept looking at it."

Susan's heart pounded. "Why?"

"I don't know *why*. I have no idea *why*." She turned back to the toilet.

"But you were there... *there*," Brianne said.

"So?"

"Did you see it? Did you see what happened?"

"Well, I'd just walked by, taking a load off if you know what I mean. I turned, and I saw that girl falling to the ground."

"Then why..."

Veronica's fat face turned as white as a sheet. "Because I was supposed to be working. *Working*. And that girl fell dead practically at my feet. And... a boy was screaming."

"You told the police then."

"No, I was long gone from the area when they came over to look at the body. They didn't think to ask me anything. There was a big crowd and I went back to my work."

Susan didn't know what to say. A large lump had grown in her throat and her daughter appeared frazzled to say the least at the woman's final report.

"Did you see anything else?" Susan finally asked.

Veronica flushed the toilet and turned to them both. "No. Now, if you don't mind, I need to get back to work. You don't have a boss like I have."

More Clues

Somewhat geared up for another day at school, Brianne had already made her way to the bus. Oscar had followed close behind. Henry was sick. Tomorrow would be another visit to the doctor's and Susan wasn't sure she even wanted to go. Dr. Randolph would tell them the same thing. Either he wasn't eating right, or he wasn't getting enough sleep. Was he exercising, doing anything to improve his health?

It was early morning, and the skies were gray as Susan approached the doors. She knocked once as instructed and waited. Early December was brisk, and her coat was barely keeping out the cold. She held it close to her body, leaning in to the glass. No one.

She knocked again, harder this time, and stood with her back to the door, watching the traffic. There was no one, or almost no one in the parking lot, and as Susan breathed in the air, wishing, no hoping beyond hope that a miracle would happen for her husband, a sudden jolt of the door made her jump.

She turned. A bald man in a yellow vest stared down at her. He was tall, large, and well over 6 feet tall. His mouth was twisted funny, as if he was wondering who she was. The door opened. "Yes?" he asked as Susan drew her coat even closer around her body.

"I... I have an appointment with Cecil."

He blinked at her.

"An appointment, with Cecil? Why?"

"I'm a detective."

"Your badge?"

Susan might have laughed, but as it was the situation was far from hilarious. She was standing out in the cold, her body almost frozen, and this tall, bald man was asking her if she had a badge?

"Well, no."

The door opened wider. "Figures. Come in. "

She whisked by him, shuddering. "Thanks."

A hand reached forth. "Hi, I'm Cecil. You must be Susan. The detective without a badge."

Susan smiled awkwardly.

"No matter. I've never trusted real cops or their attendants anyway." He motioned towards a door. "There's a chair in there, actually two..." He grinned. "Sitting is always preferable."

"Thanks," she said, wondering if Cecil had meant the FBI by his 'attendant' comment, preferring to wonder rather than to broach the subject with him.

She watched his large feet clunk against the Linoleum floor. Once inside, she sat on a cold, resin chair and looked over at him.

His eyes were large, the size of walnuts, and his huge hands clenched and unclenched in front of him as he watched her. Susan thought briefly how easily it would be for him to snap a broom handle, or her neck.

"So, what do you want to know?"

The room was stark, nothing really to speak of on the walls, just an old desk and some papers scattered across it, and two resin chairs...

"Do you know Veronica Edwards?"

"Sure as I'm sitting here."

"She tells me she saw the girl fall. Where were you at the time of the murder?"

"I ah...saw Veronica but just briefly. I was there too. I saw the girl fall."

"Before that, what was the deceased doing?"

"Looking at clothing, I suppose. I had only just come upon her, through the outside door near *Clothing to Die For*, and there she was... a beauty. But she was holding her head funny. In the next minute, she was falling, and holding onto something on her head, and reaching out for the clothing rack, trying to stop herself from falling I guess."

"What did she have against her head?"

"It looked like a paper towel. It was bloody..."

"Where was the paper towel after the woman fell?"

"That part was strange..." He leaned forward. "I mean, one second, there it was and the next she was on the ground without it. It wasn't anywhere I could see. And there was that child, screaming."

"How did you know the girl was stabbed?"

"She wasn't wearing any shoes. There was one that had fallen out of her hand, but she wasn't wearing it obviously. I just sort of put two and two together."

"Did you see anyone near her?"

"Everyone. Tons of people."

"Did you hear about the blood found in the women's bathroom?"

"And all the missing paper towels? Yes. All of us on staff here have been talking about it, trying to figure out – who did it."

"So, what have you come up with?"

"Her sister that's who."

Susan imagined the wad in Katrine's hand along with the shoe, the blood kept safe and un-dripping within it, and how she must have hidden it behind her until everyone had cleared out. But the police had arrived, and fairly quickly, so how had she managed it?

"Veronica says that she saw a hand reach out to grab it," Susan stated, hoping the man would tell her more.

"Yeah, it freaked her out, I can tell you. Just after it happened I found her trembling in the office."

***

"You don't have to come."

Henry was pale. He took her arm as they walked to the car.

"You can't be serious. I can't let you drive the car in this condition."

She opened the door and he slid in.

"I suppose you're right. I'm sorry, Susan."

"I'm just sorry I can't help you with much more than a taxi service."

She slid in the driver's side and started the car.

Henry was silent for most of the trip, and Susan wondered what he was thinking about. It was bad enough to know what she was thinking about. But she must remain strong for Henry.

She turned on the radio. A tune, one of their favorites, suddenly blared in her ears. She turned down the volume and stopped at the first light. "I'm sorry, too," she began. "But Henry, you've got to eat better, and get more exercise than you're getting."

"Yes, doc."

She turned to look at him. Even with his pale face and hollow eyes, his hair was still that beautiful red, like the entrails of a large fish. She would make this work. Maybe, just maybe she'd been spending too many hours looking for Roxy's killer. It was time to give up this goose chase and spend more time with him. The truth of her thoughts melted into her bones, her heart. If they didn't find a donor soon her dear Henry would die.

Turning off the radio, she listened to his breathing as she drove, listened for problems, for anything. All she really knew was they'd been waiting for almost three months to get a new heart without success. Maybe now?

***

Time had stopped for Susan. After checking the strength of Henry's heartbeat and blood pressure, the doctor had suggested a mechanical pump. But perhaps 'suggested' was a poor word. What the doctor had demanded was the implantation — something to keep his heart going until the transplant could take place. It sounded almost alien, even to Susan, who had spent the majority of the last few months searching out the murderer of someone she didn't even know and her daughter had met for only a few brief seconds.

What was wrong with her?

Henry was dying!

A fresh tear dripped down her left cheek. The room was dark and her Henry was asleep. And she was alone.

***

"You're letting the murder – drop?"

For whatever reason, Henry looked better the following morning, though he hadn't awakened until after 10 a.m.

"We have to."

He stood up and met her at the foot of the bed. Taking her hands, he looked deeply into her eyes. "I love you, but I need to work."

"But..."

"I *need* to work."

"But..."

"No buts. We will find the killer, you and me together, with the help of our pretty persuasive daughter. And when this is all over, we'll take a break."

"What sort of break?"

"You know. A break. I'll get my heart transplant, and rest up and do whatever the bloody..."

"You call that a break?"

"It is for me." He smiled and kissed her full on the lips. She closed her eyes, taking it in, trying to recall that first day when he'd come to her door asking for a cup of sugar. The first time she'd laid eyes on his apartment. Those silly resin chairs...

"Cecil. He really creeped me out."

"I told you not to go alone, remember?"

"No, I don't remember. And besides..." She kissed him lightly on the lips. "I found out who killed Roxy."

"You what?" He blinked at her, his thoughts wildly still on her. This she knew.

"A man grabbed for that paper towel. Once Roxy hit the floor, it was a man's hand that reached out to take away the evidence."

"Who's hand?"

"A man's. I told you!"

"Who? What man?"

"Probably that Fred...Cardigan."

"So... he removed evidence."

Susan was stumped. "I can't believe you're taking this so calmly."

"Why shouldn't I?" He stroked her hair.

"Because...because you shouldn't. It's a clue!"

"Okay, so it was a man." He touched her face. "You are so beautiful; do you know that?"

She must have blushed. He laughed. "Look, it's great that you know that a man took the paper towel. He was more than likely trying to hide the

62

fact that Roxanne had been murdered in the bathroom. But so, what? He probably isn't the killer."

"Why do you say that?"

"How could the man be in the women's bathroom and then suddenly present himself in perfect condition some ten minutes later, give or take, at *Clothing to Die For*? It's just not possible."

"Then what is possible?"

She stared up at him as his hands found her waist. "He was helping the killer."

Susan's heart jumped. "Right. That makes sense. "

He kissed her lightly on the neck.

"Okay, so..." she crooned, "we need to go over to Fred's and talk to him again. Obviously, he's not telling us everything."

"I know, but we can't do that now."

"Why not? It's morning and the kids are in school and..."

"Honestly, Susan. Do you really think I want to do that at a time like this?"

"Are you sure. I mean, your heart."

"Now look. I've got to watch what I eat. I have to take care of myself and get those raunchy tests. I even get to have that weird VAD put inside my chest, don't I deserve to have a little fun — you know, get some exercise?"

She laughed. "I don't think that's what the doctor had in mind."

He nibbled her ear. "Who cares?" he mumbled.

***

"I forgot something."

The next evening Susan got a strange call from Cecil. He thanked her first for coming out in the terrible weather to visit with him, as if she'd paid him a social call or something, and then he told her something that did more than open her ears.

"That Sadie. She is always so controlling. After I found Veronica in the office crying and shaking, Mrs. Chartreuse came in and she pulled us apart. 'I won't have any of that here' she said, as if we were doing something wrong. I don't know about you, but this Veronica is something to be admired because of her kindness. Treat the woman with respect, and she has no reason to look down on you."

"Veronica comes from a hard background and that Chartreuse woman has no idea what living that sort of life feels like. The only reason she works at Inglewood is to get the free stuff and to save up enough money to return to England where her family is."

Susan hadn't noticed any sort of accent coming from Sadie, but remained silent.

"Mrs. Chartreuse might be the perfect picture of everything, but her heart is as cold as ice. Ice, I tell you. She probably killed that girl. I could see her doing it, too, even though my biggest suspicions run to the murder victim's sister."

"What makes you think Katrine could kill anyone?"

"Have you seen her anger?"

Susan recalled the anger of one Veronica Edwards, but decided to remain silent.

"And then there's Sadie. We can't do anything right. She is in total control and tells us when we've miss-stepped. But when she..." The words trailed off and for a moment Susan wondered if the man had decided not to share what he'd forgotten to share the day before. And then it came.

"She told us not to talk to the police – that they wouldn't understand."

"Understand what?"

"Since you're not the police, I figured I could speak up." Susan could almost see him smiling. "I asked her the same thing. She said, 'We need to make sure people feel safe having their meetings and events here. We can't worry them that another murder might take place.' It was so funny. She's a worker like us, albeit a glorified one, so why does she care who decides to rent out the space?"

"I told her that I wasn't going to talk to anyone. I needed my job, and besides, I really didn't care one way or the other about the dead girl. But after she left, I realized that I really did care. When you asked to speak with me, my first thought was, 'maybe now I can finally speak.' I'd heard you weren't a real cop, just sort of a pretend one working with your husband..."

Susan took a deep breath. "Anything else?" she asked.

"Yeah, I didn't tell you about the free stuff."

"Go ahead."

"Well, because she works where she does, she gets kudos that far escapes the rest of us; though you can be sure everyone else knows about it and resents her for it. Imagine getting free items from the vendors, free tickets and who knows what else, simply because you're the head cleaner?"

Katrine

The moment was awkward. Almost like visiting with a boss, your head whirling about all the things you might have done wrong. Only in the case with Katrine, it was more like your mind was whirling with what she could possibly be thinking to give the answers she did, her parents looking on as if what she was saying was the most natural thing in the world.

"You what?"

"Dated him."

"You dated Johnny?"

Katrine looked at Susan as if she was the one from the strange planet. "Sure. I never back out on a dare."

"So, she dared you to date him?" Henry's words were static, almost as if he was saying them without really saying them.

"She dared me to do lots of things. Actually, the dares went both ways." Katrine looked over at her parents. They weren't smiling. "Most of the dares no one knows about."

"On that first date Johnny, well... we kissed a lot. He seemed eager to kiss and it was hard to get him to stop. I later found out he was merely trying to compare my kisses with my sisters — as if she knew how to do it right." Katrine paused, and looked again briefly at her parents who were still silent.

They'd been welcomed in to the home, almost quietly, if that's possible. Without more than a nod and a wave of the hand, Mrs. Anderson had directed them again to the living room, her husband, Craig following behind her. They'd scheduled the little interview over the phone, when Katrine could be home, but there was some underlying factor that crept under Susan's skin as she spoke with her. Almost as if the family had had an argument right before the door had opened.

"I was so mad. I thought she was tired of him, you know. I really liked him after that first date and told her I wanted to go on another, but she wouldn't have it. Said it was all a joke, to see what Johnny was made of. I promised myself that I would get back at her for making me look like a fool."

"Did Johnny know?"

"About the set-up? More than likely. He called me up and asked me out. I was worried about my sister. He said they'd broken up. He said he always liked me better anyway. Roxy didn't get upset when I told her all about it, so I figured everything was okay. And it felt like it too, until I found out what was really going on."

"And that was?" Susan asked.

"A set up. I was set up."

"But why, for what purpose?" Henry asked. He was looking better today; his red hair parted evenly, his face calm, healthy. For a week now, he'd been doing better and Susan wondered if that meant he wouldn't need the VAD device after all.

"Just a joke. But it didn't make sense to me at all. I was so mad. I started spreading lies around campus. It was stupid, but I told people that my sister was as fake as a plastic doll. Sure, she acted like everyone was important to her, but she really didn't mean it. I was the meanest to Johnny. He'd really ticked me off. Every time he saw me he'd say, 'There she is, the best kisser on the planet.' He'd say it loudly, so everyone within earshot would hear it, and those who did would laugh. Sure, it was first grade, the attitude, you know, but I was just so mad. Everything came to a halt after I told everyone that I could think of that he had gotten my sister pregnant."

"How did your sister feel about that?"

"Pretty ticked off." Katrine looked again at her parents. "When Mom and Dad found out what I'd been doing they pulled me out of college. I felt like a two-year-old. Who pulls their daughter out of school for standing up for herself?"

Craig opened his mouth, and then closed it.

"I mean, it wasn't even *my* fault. I didn't start this mess, but somehow, as in always, I am left holding the bag. It's just not fair." Katrine's eyes glistened hotly. "So now I have to get a job, I can't finish school, and my life sucks."

"And Johnny?"

"Him? He just walks around as if he hasn't done anything. I see this... this stupid counselor. She asks me all these questions, and I just hate her!"

"Katrine!"

"Sorry, Dad, but you know what, I hate living here, and I hate the control, and I hate you!" Katrine stood, wiping some imaginary dust off of her jeans and brushing a stray tear from her cheek. "I'm glad she's dead. Dead, dead, dead!"

Katrine left the room, young Kent peeking around the stairway where the girl had fled.

"What happened?" he asked.

"Nothing to worry yourself about, son. Come on in and join us."

Susan smiled over at him and Henry waved his hand. "Yeah, we haven't talked to you yet."

Susan knew Henry had had no plans when it came to talking to the eight-year-old. Still, it was a sweet gesture, something they all needed to refocus on after the attack of Katrine.

But the boy wasn't smiling when he stepped into the living room and sat down by his parents. In fact, it looked like he'd been crying. He cuddled next to his mother, and as she wrapped her slim arm around him, he buried his head in her lap.

"I'm sorry, son," Craig began, but the boy reared up and glared at him.

"You're not sorry! My sister is dead!"

Craig leaned closer to his son, but the boy only pushed against his leg.

"You, you are a liar!" he railed.

The man hadn't said anything that could even be interpreted as a lie.

"Son, I..."

"Don't call me that. I hate you!"

Shoeless

She'd spent the entire morning following the footsteps of Johnny's places of travel before she saw him. He was heading her way, his blonde hair flattened against his face. No spikes today. A girl was at his side, but it wasn't Matty Slack.

Susan stepped in front of him.

"Oh, it's you."

"That's right. We need to talk."

The tall brunette smiled over at her.

"I can't. I'll be late for class."

"Just a few minutes. I need to ask you about Matty." She'd meant to ask him about Roxanne or her sister, but the idea of a new girl on Johnny's arm had intrigued her. How many girls could this young man be interested in beyond the casual date?

The girl blinked over at him, removing her hand from his. "I thought Matty was history," she said, her eyes on fire. Her lower lip trembled, and for all intents and purposes, continued to tremble though the entire dialogue.

"She is." Johnny frowned over at Susan before turning his gaze back to the girl. "You have to believe me."

"So, how long have you two been together?" Susan suddenly wished she'd been able to bring Brianne along, but she was in school after all, and taking her away from class wouldn't help her any when it came to graduating.

"Two days. And you are –?" the girl asked.

"Susan." She reached out her hand. The girl didn't take it. "And you?"

"Cecilia. Cecil. Just call me Cecil."

"Cecil?" Susan's mind whirled. Now there was a name a person didn't hear often. Where had she heard it before, and quite recently? Cecil brushed her dark hair away from her tanned face.

"Matty and I broke up," Johnny said, looking into Susan's eyes.

"Why?"

"None of your business."

"Where did you meet Cecil?" she asked.

The girl brightened. "Oh, we've known each other for a long, long time. Only he —"

"Like I said, I'm no longer dating Matty. Anything else?"

"Why did you date Katrine?"

"Who?" Johnny asked, though his skin paled.

"Roxanne's sister. Katrine says it was a dare."

"Oh, that."

"You dated Katrine?" Cecil looked visibly shocked. "You didn't tell me that! She's as crazy as, I don't know, but she's crazy!"

Johnny blushed. "Look, I didn't know it was her, okay? Roxy seemed different, that's all, and I figured she was just having a bad day. Look. Don't get mad. But she was weird, you know. All she wanted to do was... well, anyway, she was just weird. Later, I found out that Roxy had played a joke on me. She wanted to see if I could tell the difference. She told me I shouldn't have kissed her..."

"You—kissed her?" Cecil was a wave of emotion. Flailing her hands, she bent her head toward the ground, her lower lip still trembling. "I knew it, I just knew it! And so, you're just going to date me a couple of weeks, is that it? And then, you're going to drop me like you've done with almost every other girl at this stupid college!"

"No! You're different."

"Different, how?"

"You're...you're smart and funny and..."

"How is my kissing, huh? Does it compare to Katrine's or her sister's? And Matty, how did she kiss?"

"I... I don't know!"

Susan was suddenly embarrassed. Why was she always digging into the can of worms as if she knew something about it? If only Brianne was here, maybe she'd be able to calm them both down. She might have laughed in just that moment, but she couldn't. They were fighting full-force now, and,

70

in fact, had forgotten that she was standing there. The rampage continued. Minutes that seemed like hours ticked by. And then Cecil looked over at her. "I know who you are," she said icily. "You're that detective mother! I saw you at the craft fair. I almost walked up, but I thought it might be better if I didn't. Now I know why."

"I know who you are as well," Susan said, staring the girl down. "You work at the fairgrounds."

Cecil glared over at Johnny. "I think we're done," she said.

***

Susan's hands trembled as she reached for the doorknob of *True and Vine*. She hadn't set an appointment with Justine, but there was a question she had to ask, and the question couldn't wait. She sat in the adjoining waiting area, and, as the minutes ticked, Susan watched the clock. Ten-fifteen-twenty.

The receptionist, a short, stocky woman, had suggested she'd have to be patient. She would contact Ms. Commons when the woman had finished with her guest. A half-an-hour later, Justine emerged from the adjoining room. A woman Susan didn't recognize was with her. They parted ways with a handshake.

Justine smiled over at her. "So, you have more questions. Do you want to talk here or inside my office?"

"In your office, if that's alright," Susan offered.

Justine wore pink, from shoes to top, and as Susan entered her office, the same pelican stared over at her from its frame. She looked once again at the cup holder, the stapler and other desk supplies that sat in the same places she had first seen them.

"So, what can I do for you?" the woman asked, sitting in her high-backed roller chair.

Susan found a cushioned chair in front of the desk and sat. Her eyes drifted again to the pelican.

"I... uh, so I'm needing some information about some of your employees; the ones who clean the facilities at Inglewood Fair Grounds."

"What do you want to know?" She smiled easily over at Susan, and reached for a pink pen. "I'm pretty busy today, so you'll have to make it quick."

"Sure. I've spoken with Mrs. Chartreuse. Sadie. I've also learned that a Cecilia works at Inglewood."

"Yes."

"And she also goes by Cecil?"

"Of course, oh, I see. It's confusing, I know, but the older, bald man, that's Cecil. The girl, also Cecil — she doesn't like the nickname Cecilia and prefers if you don't use it – was also there. Cecil, the man, may have been there too that night, but he usually works alone — he primarily takes care of the floors and light bulbs and such, and lets the others do the bathroom cleanings."

Susan breathed a sigh of relief. So, there were two Cecil's working at Inglewood, and if two Cecil's, then an additional suspect. Her thoughts drifted to Fred Cardigan. Hadn't the man, Cecil, said that a man had reached out to grab the paper towel just when Roxanne had fallen dead to the floor? Who was this man? It was time to ask Fred some questions.

***

Fred was knee deep in boxes. It was late afternoon, Henry was taking a nap, and Brianne had decided to come with her. She'd practically jumped at the chance.

"Are we going to see that old guy, the one who owns the clothing store?" she asked.

"Yes. But I want you to be careful about what you say."

"Why?"

"I don't know – it's just a feeling I get when I'm around him."

"Okay."

With the door opened, Susan searched the room only briefly until Fred's head popped up from behind one of the boxes. The place was strewn with clothing, though nothing yet had been put on the racks. The racks were empty. They shone a silver glow as she and her daughter walked past boxes, finally stopping at the cash register. Like before, there weren't any customers.

"Oh, uh, why didn't you call? I'm trying to get the clothing ready."

The place was a mess – even more so this time, if that were possible. If the man didn't want customers in his store, why had he left the door unlocked? There seemed to be nothing hanging up, and shoes, boots, belts and other clothing were strewn all along the floors between the aisles.

"Maybe we can help," Brianna offered.

Fred stumbled to them, kicking a box behind him on the way over. He wore a yellow cardigan and a matching yellow tie. His pants were a little short for his stick-thin body, but he managed to still pull off the Mr. Roger's look.

"I don't know... I don't know..." the man fumbled, looking around him. "I think I'm going to have to close this place. I just don't see how I'm going to make it work."

"Well, the place is a mess. Once it's cleaned up, people will probably want to shop here."

Fred breathed in. He looked Brianne square in the eyes. "You're a pretty gal," he said. "Want to work here?"

Brianne laughed. "No, I mean, we'd love to help you clean up, and then you can hire whoever you want."

"I should have never taken this shop from my father," he stumbled, picking up a dress and hanging it haphazardly on its hanger and then on the metal rack. "I was never meant for work like this."

"What work did you do before owning a clothing shop?"

"Oh, I worked on buildings mostly; fixed up places in need of fixing."

"What sort of buildings?"

Fred suddenly smiled. "You sure do ask a lot of questions, but I like them."

Brianne smiled back, and gingerly lifted a pair of pants from off of the floor. "Where do you want these?" she asked.

Fred pointed. And so, it went. She and Brianne were with Fred for four hours before Susan realized that it was near eight and she still hadn't asked him the questions she'd planned on asking. The place was pretty spruced up, too. It almost looked like a shop, with everything organized and the boxes flattened and shoved in the metal dumpster out back – well, except for the one hanging out in the corner.

"I can't thank you enough," Fred said, leaning against the counter and surveying the room. "Looks like a brand-new place."

Brianne laughed and patted the man on the arm. "Now, you'll need some signs," she said. "And you'll need to get this counter cleaned off."

Fred looked at her again, and Susan thought he was going to ask her to work for him again, but instead he said, "So, why are you here?"

Now he was looking straight at Susan and she was trying to remember the questions that had once melded within her brain. They seemed silly now, though she knew they needed to be asked. "We are searching for the killer of Roxanne Anderson. I have a couple of questions about that."

"Shoot."

"Well, the girl was holding a paper towel against her head. We're thinking she was stabbed in the lady's restroom, found the paper towels, and hobbled to your spot before finally collapsing. While she fell, someone grabbed for the paper towel. Do you know who that might have been?"

Fred paled. "I have no idea," he said.

Was Fred smiling? A sudden weirdness felt its way up Susan's back. Just like before, she couldn't place why, but this man sure gave her the creeps. Suddenly, the second question she had planned on asking him was no longer necessary.

***

The place smelled of fresh grease. Oscar was at the table biting into a hamburger. He looked up when he saw them. "We'll I'll be... Dad, guess who finally decided to make their way home?"

It was near nine when she and Brianne finally stepped through the front door. After leaving Fred, they had traveled home, stopping once at a fast food restaurant to eat, and then taking the side streets in order to talk privately about the strange Mr. Cardigan.

"Honey! Where have you two been? I've been worried sick! Why didn't you answer your phone?" The words blasted in Susan's ears. She stumbled for an answer.

"We... I..."

"Dad, you wouldn't believe what we found out about Fred Cardigan. That guy is a real weirdo." She removed her coat, laying it over one of the kitchen chairs. Sitting down, she removed her shoes, all the while still talking as if the process was the most natural thing in the world. As Susan stood, agape, her daughter spelled out the entire weird episode.

"Fred was lying through his teeth! He told us that he knew nothing about the bloody paper towel. But it just had to be him." She walked over to the stove. "Can I have it?" she asked.

Henry nodded.

"Gads, Dad! This guy's place looked like a tornado had hit it. There were clothes everywhere! He hadn't done anything but empty the boxes and all of the stuff was just thrown everywhere. Me and Mom, we helped him clean it up..." She reached for the bun and placing a hamburger patty inside, felt for the catsup. "Ask Mom, she'll tell you."

"Susan?"

Susan looked over at Henry. He was livid, his face matching his hair. She glanced briefly at Oscar who was taking another bite of his hamburger.

"Sorry. We just got side-tracked."

"For five hours?"

"Wow. Dad, don't get mad. Mom probably accidently turned her phone off. Right, Mom?"

Susan reached inside her purse. Her coat was still on and she hadn't removed her shoes nor had she begun to fix her hamburger—which she wouldn't have done anyway. Hadn't she and Brianne just eaten? Her cell phone was on mute. "Sorry," she said again.

"See, Mom's sorry." Brianne sat down and took a bite of her hamburger. "What did you guys have to drink? Oh, fries!" she wailed, grabbing for a few stragglers still in the middle of the table on a plate.

"Milk."

Susan watched her husband. Was that a small smile trying to find its way into the corner of his mouth? She thought of Fred then, trying not to smile when it was obvious to her and to Brianne as they'd talked about the incident in the car that the man was trying to hide something.

"Hungry?" he asked.

"No." Susan took off her coat and sat on the closest chair to the kitchen door.

"Well then, why do you suspect this Fred character, besides the fact that he's more than likely hid some evidence?"

"Exactly!" Brianne sang. "Why would he hide it? Why, Dad?"

"Because he was mortified, overcome by the scene. He was scared out of his wits, that's why."

"You should have been here! That man was lying through his teeth, right Mom?" She took another bite.

"Right."

"I think he has something to do with this murder. I don't know how he could have killed her in the bathroom when he was at his booth, but he was purposely trying to hide evidence so whoever killed her wouldn't be caught. Think of it, Dad!"

"I am thinking of it. And I was worried about you two."

"Yeah," Oscar mumbled between another bite of hamburger. "Me, too."

Susan smiled. She couldn't help it. "You, too?" she prodded.

"Yeah, and if that guy is as big of a creep as Brianne has made him out to be, you may have never come home!"

"You don't really think..."

"I think you might just be on to something," Henry said. "If that man is merely playing the fool, who knows what he is really like; what if this business, *Clothing to Die For*, isn't really what he purports it to be?"

"Purports?"

"Yes. Maybe he wants everyone to think that *Clothing to Die* For is some sort of legitimate business. Did you check out the back room?"

"No." Brianne was suddenly pale. "Don't you find it strange, Dad, that he was going through all of those clothing boxes and throwing everything on the floor? Why would he do that?"

"Maybe he was looking for something other than clothes."

Susan's heart stopped. "Like what?"

***

"I don't think I like wandering around in the dark," Brianne said, tucking the quickly fading flashlight into her coat pocket.

"Shhh, now remember, we're just going to search the outside premises."

"Why? I bet he has the shoe inside."

"There's probably an alarm. And besides, I don't want you getting hurt."

"It's late. The guy is probably home by now."

"But what if he isn't?" Henry looked at her suddenly. "Maybe we should have left her home."

"I heard that, and anyway, you need me. I'm the only one here who's young enough to climb up to that second story window."

"What —"

Brianne was already pointing up. I can climb on that garbage can there, get to the roof, and swing in."

"Swing — in?"

"Sure, Mom, it's easy."

"Easy." She looked over at Henry.

"Your life is more likely to be over easy if you go that route."

"Funny, Dad."

"I'm serious. We don't know if Fred's place has a burglar alarm system. Even if the windows aren't wired, something inside might be. Let's just stick to our plan. Check the grounds around the business for clues, the dumpster, anything outside."

"Gads, you guys are no fun! But okay."

Susan breathed in a sigh of relief. They checked the cement pad behind the store and found nothing more than litter—pop cans, paper. Even the trash yielded no results.

"So, what do you think?" Brianne asked, holding up what looked like an old, worn suitcase. Susan was tired and she knew Henry wouldn't be able to take much more of this fruitless search in the dark. Susan shined her flashlight in the direction of her daughter.

"Gads, Mom! My eyes!"

"Sorry. Undo the clasp."

"That's what I'm trying to do."

Susan couldn't help it; as her daughter fumbled to open the suitcase, she remembered, and not too fondly, of her own experience in a similar trashcan looking for clues during the *Scrambled* case. At least her search had been during the daytime.

"It's not coming apart!" she shrieked, when, moments later, the case still remained shut.

"Let me try," Henry offered, stepping over to his daughter through the muck inside the trashcan; a sort of boom-slush sound echoed throughout the can.

"I think the lock is bent." Henry reached into his pocket and pulled out a piece of wire. At least, that's what it looked like to Susan.

"Come on, Dad! You can do it."

Susan smiled to herself watching father and daughter. It was almost like watching a *Laurel and Hardy* movie of long ago. Finally, when Susan

77

thought the attempt fruitless, a small wail escaped her daughter's lips. The case plunked open, revealing something inside.

"What is it?" Susan asked, her heart pounding suddenly, her lips dry.

And then she saw it, something about the size of a shoe, wrapped in some sort of paper, hoisted above her husband's head, and he was blinking at her, trying to shield his eyes from the light as he spoke to her: "Honey, I think this is it. I think we've found the shoe."

Gifts

"Dad, we found it! The shoe and the chunk of paper towels!"

Holding the suitcase in his lap, they all looked inside, not daring to touch the two items that lay there. They were still in the car, parked some two blocks from *Clothing to Die For*. It had taken all Susan had to watch Brianne carry that suitcase to the car.

"I don't know about you, but I'm not going to clasp the lock. We had a hard enough time getting the thing loose the first time."

"Right." Susan looked at the clock that had recently been repaired in the car. *12:45* it read.

Henry had already placed the opened suitcase in the back seat next to Brianne. She was eyeing it warily. "Now, remember not to touch it. We'll leave it here, in the back, until tomorrow. We have to. In the morning, I'll take it to the police station."

Brianne was frowning. "You can't do that, Dad. You can't."

"Why not? He turned from her and started the ignition.

"The cops will think you did it. Your fingerprints are all over that case."

Susan laughed.

"What's so funny?"

"You. Your Dad's prints are there, but his aren't the only ones."

"That's right. The killer's prints are on that case. And on the shoes. And on the bloody paper towel. Sorry," Brianne said.

"No need to be sorry. Tomorrow we'll know who the killer is once and for all," Susan said.

***

Officer Crump rubbed his bald head. As Henry, Susan, and Brianne stood as silently as possible next to the opened case, the gloved man looked over the contents at the front desk.

"You found this, where?" the officer asked.

"In the dumpster behind *Clothing to Die For*."

"What were you doing over there?"

"I have a detective business now..."

"And you say this is the shoe that Roxanne Anderson was killed with?"

"It was black. A stiletto. It was wrapped up with a piece of paper towel."

Susan looked down at the bloodied paper towel and shoe. Both held distinct bloody fingerprints, and Susan wondered what the final results would reveal. Was Fred Cardigan the murderer of Roxanne Anderson? And if not the murderer, was he in league with someone else?

The officer lifted the case. "Thank you for your help," he said. "We'll look these over, Henry. How are you, anyway? Folks here say the force isn't the same without you. Chief Gregson especially."

"Is he here? Maybe—"

"Nope. On vacation." The man smiled, revealing a missing front tooth. "Look. Don't worry. We'll check out the blood here with forensics. You know the drill. We have some officers already handling the homicide area. We'll let you know if we have any more questions."

***

"I told you Dad, we shouldn't have taken those things in. You're a detective after all, and it should be your find."

"But I needed to have the blood checked. And it will only help us to have others searching as we are for the killer."

"But they won't give you any credit. It will be like all of the other times with Mom."

Susan's heart stopped. Her daughter was more than likely right. When had Henry ever received any credit for his work; when had *she*? And how could they be sure that the information on the blood would be revealed as soon as the results became available?

"Actually," Henry offered, taking off his coat, "they will have to be in touch with me. We're all in this together now. Our next step is to call the Andersons and let them know that their daughter's shoe has been discovered."

***

May Anderson was crying uncontrollably. "So, it's really true then, she's been murdered."

Susan blinked in her direction. Brianne was silent, her husband looking past their heads. Isn't this why they were searching for the truth? But perhaps the woman had secretly hoped for a different result? Like what?

"You need to know that the police are doing all they can now."

"I know...I know," May sniffed, looking up for the first time at Henry.

"We will find out who did this. And when we do, they'll get their just desserts."

"You make it sound like a real treat." May smiled slightly, and reached over for her husband's hand. Craig was silent.

"Well, we'll go then," Susan said, standing.

"Yes. Thank you for coming." Craig's hand shot out suddenly, grasping Susan's tightly. Releasing his grip, he shook Henry's. He led them to the door.

"Let us know if you learn anything else."

"We will." For the first time since arriving, Susan's thoughts drifted to Katrine. She was sitting on the couch next to her brother. Both were reading. They didn't even look up as they left them.

***

As the days turned colder, Susan continued to ask her husband if he'd heard anything from the precinct, but his answer was always no.

Plus, now that she had children, the simple Christmases that she and her husband had had previously had been replaced by all of the electronic gizmos only teens could want. Still, she was happy to finally share in Christmas with children legally hers.

"So?" she asked Henry after it was obvious he'd been speaking with someone at the police station. "What's the verdict?"

She was sitting in the living room, her movie suddenly muted.

"You're not going to like it," he said, sitting down on the couch.

"What is it, Mom?" Brianne asked, no longer angry that she'd turned the sound down. Oscar was out on a date; his second in a week. No one had met the girl yet.

Henry wiped his fingers through his red hair. "The bloody fingerprints on the shoe belong to Katrine."

"And the suitcase?"

"Only mine were found."

"I knew it!" Brianne squealed. She stood up and flailing her hands, danced around the room.

"Come on – Katrine?" Susan asked.

"That's what forensic is saying. They called the girl in last week; got some prints...they match up."

"I feel sick..."

"Mom, it just makes sense! Those two must have been angry at each other over that boy, what's his name."

"Johnny."

"Yeah."

"But could Katrine have killed her sister?"

"Sure. There was a girl at my school who killed herself because her boyfriend broke up with her."

The words made Susan sick. "I can't believe it," she said.

"Believe it." Henry reached for her hand. "I can't even imagine what her parents are going through."

"Oh, gosh. Henry..."

"I know, I know. But they have to know."

"Where is she?" Brianne asked.

"In jail; I'll call the Andersons tomorrow. They could use our support."

The Call

Henry paced. It was the morning after the visit with Katrine's parents and as Susan watched the process, trying to figure out what was going on this time, she finally opted to be silent. She was on the bed, and the make-shift office was getting more crowded by the day. Brianne and Oscar were at school, and she was in waiting mode for Henry's final declaration.

"What?" she finally asked, irritation welling in her own voice. "What?"

"I just can't believe it!"

"What?"

Henry was breathing heavily and Susan worried for him. What if the man collapsed in their bedroom? What if he fell dead at her very feet?

She stood, and walking up to him, began to shake his shoulders. "Henry, Henry!" she screamed. "What — is it?"

His shoulders shuddered under her firm hands, and tears had begun to spill from his cheeks. "I have a donor," he whispered.

"Your heart?"

"My heart."

She held him close. "We have to go – now."

"You mean right now?"

He chuckled softly. "Yes."

"Who? I mean..."

"Car accident. Where's my bag?"

They'd been preparing for this moment for months and finally it was here. The timing was horrible but it was here. "I'll get it. You just get to the car. Can you make it?" The VAD chest insertion was only a week away, but now it looked like they'd be bypassing this step, if one could call getting hooked up to a machine a step until it was time for a heart transplant – a step. A new heart? She could hardly believe it herself.

Henry pressed his warm lips to her cheek. "I love you," he said, withdrawing from her. Susan rushed to the bedroom closet and retrieved the small bag.

***

"I have to do what?"

The nurse was patient; Susan could see that, her articulation smooth, her hands quiet as she explained what was going to happen next. "We will be doing some of the same tests again, those you had on your first assessment. We want to make sure that your transplant will go as planned."

Susan tried to breathe evenly.

"After that we'll need to shave and bathe you."

"You've got to be kidding."

Doctor Richards didn't even blush. "Yes, and while we're in process, your donor heart will be examined."

"I thought you said I had a heart."

"You do, but like you, the heart must go through one more pass. Don't worry."

Susan reached for Henry, taking his arm. "I'll be here the entire time," she said.

He looked over at her, and blushing, kissed her lightly on the lips. "I know."

"I've already told the kids to make themselves at home tonight. I'll go by in the morning and make sure everything is a-okay there, and then I'll return."

"You don't need to do that."

"Yes, I do." Even as she said the words, she hope – no prayed – that Oscar would be smart, that he and Brianne would stay home.

So, the heart had come from out-of-state, and though Susan wanted to know more, other things had managed to take a higher priority, so little was currently known about the donor.

"Once we have confirmation that your heart is good to go, we'll get you set up with anesthesia. Fair enough?"

Henry nodded, though his skin had paled, and he was constantly fussing with his hospital gown. As he fussed, Doctor Richards explained in greater detail about the operation itself. Two hours later, after all of the tests, and finding the donor heart to be suitable, it was time.

As Susan sat in the waiting area, checking the clock, trying to keep her mind on the magazine she'd removed from the table, and searching her own heart for answers to the sudden operation she'd tried to prepare herself for, she realized Henry hadn't called the Andersons. There'd been no time. And now she was here, and every moment she was thinking of Henry, worrying over Henry.

But Henry would want her to call.

She breathed uneasily, realizing for the first time that she didn't have the number. She'd have to get it tonight, after the operation, when she knew Henry was okay – after that. Her eyes peered down once more into the magazine where everything floated beneath her. She'd read the same paragraph three times already. Closing the magazine and laying it on the table, she searched the room for something to eat. But she couldn't eat, could she?

She felt nauseous anyway.

Brushing a few stray tears from her eyes, she thought of her mother, but only briefly. How could she call her at a time like this? But her mother didn't even know she was in the hospital with Henry. She'd never even told her he was on the transplant list.

***

"Susan?"

"I'm sorry Mrs. Anderson."

The woman sniffed. "I know. I've been crying all night. What am I supposed to do without my little Katy?" As one hour and then two had come and gone, Susan had discovered, quite surprisingly, the Andersons' number in her purse. Now she wouldn't have to wait.

"How is Kent?"

"Quiet, but otherwise, okay. He keeps asking me when his sister is coming home."

"I'm sorry. What can I do?"

"Nothing. What can anyone do? I thought the therapy sessions were working. She seemed quiet, but other than that, everything seemed to be going fine – well, as fine as it can…"

"What's the next step for Katrine?"

"Court proceedings I guess. I just can't believe my Katy would kill… I mean, she seemed to be doing fine. Thank you for all of the help you have given us. I just didn't think…"

Susan's thoughts drifted to her husband's hospital bed. It would be some hours yet before he was finished and recovering in his room. She understood about thinking things would be one way, and then having them turn out completely different. She prayed in her heart that everything would be alright with Henry. She thought again of her mother. She would be angry if she didn't call, but…

"Susan?"

"Yes." In that moment, Susan realized she'd been daydreaming. The woman on the other end was crying uncontrollably.

"You must be busy. Thank you for calling. I've already mailed the check. Thank your husband for me, will you?"

"Sure."

"I must go now." There was a click.

***

"Mom, is Dad out yet?"

Susan looked up at the clock. It was near noon. He'd been in the operating room four hours.

"Anytime now," she lied, hoping in the lie that a part of her was telling the truth. When *would he* be finished?

Henry had been her soul mate since his first introduction to her at the *Hotel Camaro*. She smiled as she thought of the resin chairs, his only living room furniture, and the way that Ms. Boaz hadn't trusted him, or so she'd told her. And now she was gone and her son, Henry, was lying on the operating table getting a new heart.

"Mom?"

"Sorry, Brianne. What were you saying?"

"You're spaced out. Are you okay?"

Her children were still in school, but with a lunch break came opportunity. Oscar hadn't managed a call that she could see, but Brianne had.

"Fine. Don't worry. How is school?" she asked.

"Fine. I'm worried about you, Mom."

"Don't."

"What about Dad?"

"He'll more than likely be okay in a few more days."

"Do you think he's gonna die?" she asked.

Susan couldn't believe she'd asked the question. But then again, she could. She'd thought about nothing else for hours now.

"Maybe you can get some time alone, when you get home," Susan said. "I'll call you when Dad gets out of surgery and we can talk about what we're going to do tomorrow."

"I can miss school."

"No, you can't."

"Gads...Mom."

"Don't be gadding me. Where's your brother?"

"How should I know? We have different lunch times."

"Oh."

"Mom?"

"What?"

"I love you. No matter what happens."

Susan thought of all of the variables. Yes, she could lose her husband. He could be in this hospital for weeks. He might never be the same.

"Call your grandma. Tell her that Henry is in for a heart transplant," she finally said.

"You mean she doesn't know?"

"No."

"I can't believe..."

"Just call her. Will you do that?"

There was a long pause. Finally, when Susan was about to ask if she was still there, the words came. "I would do anything for you, Mom, you know that. But this is your mom. I think you should call her yourself."

Susan blinked, tears spilling from the corners of her eyes, tears she didn't even know were there.

"You're probably right."

"Grandma is weird; everybody knows that, but Mom, you need to call her. I know you two don't get along, but you always make me and Oscar work things out."

Rude Awakening

The world was an empty void. Susan blinked, trying to keep herself in check. What was the doctor saying?

"There were some complications."

Susan, who had been standing, sat back down. She hadn't yet called her mother.

The doctor's hand shot out in front of him. It reached for her shoulder. "No worries now. Your husband is fine. We expect him to be here at least a week, but if two weeks are required…"

"How soon can I see him?"

The doctor looked down at his watch. "In the next hour or so. We have a ventilator on him now; he should be able to breathe on his own soon, but don't be upset by all of the monitors and the catheter. Normal procedure." He smiled and removed his hand from her shoulder.

Tears had touched her lips. She wiped them now.

"The worst is over. Now, we will need to give your husband some time for healing."

She nodded, though it was hard for her to take in all that that would require. They had spoken of it often, but now, now her brain could hardly work. All she could think about was Henry. She hadn't lost him.

By the time she stepped into the sterile room where Henry was lying, she still hadn't called her mother, though she had called her children during the wait and had tried to clear up her eyes, her throat, anything that would give her away to Henry that she'd been crying.

Why she wanted to hide this from him she didn't know, but she somehow wanted to be brave for him. She wanted him to see that she could stand by him and stay strong for him. If all she could do was to give him comfort, well, that's what she would do.

Her hands had already been scrubbed and she had on a tasteless green gown and face mask, when she stepped inside. As promised, gadgets galore hung above, around and in her husband, as if he was some sort of Frankenstein instead of the man she had grown to know and love. His eyes were closed, and though she'd been told that he was breathing on his own, Susan watched for the rise and fall of his chest to make sure.

She touched his hand, which seemed frail now, now that he was back with a new heart and a new start in life. He didn't move at her touch, and Susan wondered if this was because he was so deeply drugged. Had to be. Well, she would wait.

Her eyes closed before she knew it, and by the time she awakened it was 2 in the morning. She had fallen asleep in the chair, and someone had brought her a pillow and blanket. Peering over at her husband, she watched him again as he slept. She stood, moving her fingers through his red hair, now graying in spots, making a firm part with her index finger like he always wore it.

How had she first known that she loved him?

That first time at her hotel door?

Probably.

More than likely.

She smiled, her heart pounding.

She had never felt the same about Bob, not even in the beginning when she thought she'd been in love. Funny, but now that she had something to compare, she knew that she had never really loved him; it was the idea of being in love that she'd liked.

But Bob was gone, and if he'd truly ever loved her, she would never know.

His killer had been found, which brought her back to her mother and her jailed husband, William, and Roxanne Anderson, and Roxy's sister, Katrine. Could a college girl really strike out at a sister and kill her? There would come a time for more questions, but the time was not now.

"You are beautiful," Henry said.

It was more like a whisper, like a bird fluttering its wings overhead, but he had definitely spoken.

"Henry?"

"What, did you think…"

"Don't talk now."

He grinned. "I must…"

"Stop. Don't say anything. Just let me look into your eyes."

***

A day later, when Brianne and Oscar arrived at the hospital, Susan had still not called her mother. But by that time, all was forgotten, in favor of what was currently transpiring. It was all she could do to take it all in anyway.

Fever.

Fatigue.

Weight gain.

And her personal least favorite: shortness of breath, all signs of possible heart rejection.

Henry was doing better almost by the hour, and it seemed to Susan that they'd be able to leave the hospital in a week, instead of the two-week period she'd previously been given. Upon leaving, it was her duty to watch for the signs, though the doctor also said some patients had no typical signs of rejection and that was why follow-up visits were so important.

Susan hadn't even thought of Katrine by the end of the first week at the hospital with Henry, until she suddenly and quite unexpectedly was handed an envelope with the Anderson's return address on it. There was nothing she could do but read it.

Henry was sitting up. He looked over at her, whispered something in Brianne's ear, and she and Oscar left the room.

"What?" he asked when they were alone.

"The Anderson's. They've sent you a check."

"Good. We probably have more bills than we can afford to pay."

"It came with a note."

"And?"

"Are you feeling well enough? I mean…"

"Look at me. Don't I look as if I can take you out dancing this very night?"

She looked at the tubes still hooked up to his body. While some of them had been removed, his heart was still being monitored, and he was still getting some drip system into his veins.

"Well, if you think you can handle it."

"Shoot – I mean tell me what it says."

Here is the last check. I believe this is up to date. We are dealing with the separation of our daughter as only parents can – with emptiness – hoping that the charges will lead us to the truth of what really happened. She is being held without bond and I am torn between loving her and wishing I never knew she'd been a part of this. We hope our daughter gets the help she needs.

May and Craig Anderson

Susan folded the note and slipped it back inside the envelope with the check.

"I wish I could get out of this bed and help her."

"Me too."

"Maybe you can do something."

"Me?"

There was a slight knock at the door. "Can we come in yet?" Brianne asked.

As the door opened, Susan smiled at the chocolate still staining Brianne's lips.

"Come and sit by me," Henry said. "We have some things to talk about."

***

They all had assignments. Susan was to search out Fred Cardigan. Find out what he knew about the contents of the dumpster out back – surprisingly he hadn't stayed long in jail before being released, but without fingerprints... Brianne was to talk to Johnny Reimbolt, and with the assistance of her brother, maybe he would let something drop. And Oscar? It was time that they met this mystery girl. He was expected to set up a date and time for them all to meet. Of course, this date had to match Henry's coming home to the family, but it was about time that everyone worked together.

Susan left Henry's room to get something to eat. Feeling a bit winded, she made her way to the hospital cafeteria. Henry was feeling better, and with an increase of health came more opportunities, if she could call them that. Her thoughts drifted to the painful letter. Why was Henry so adamant that they help these people? They were no longer getting paid. Katrine was in jail.

But, what if Katrine isn't guilty? Henry had proposed to all of them, and she had thought upon his words. Something was missing. It wasn't motive. Katrine had every reason to murder her sister, at least in her eyes, but perhaps there was something else. She just had to trust Henry, and she needed to listen to her own instincts. She wasn't a real detective but he was. Henry actually knew what he was doing.

She thought again of her mother, wondering what she should do now. According to the doctor, her husband would be returning home within the week. Though that meant taking things easy for the most part, it still meant that she would have to leave him for extended hours if she was back on the case. The only thing that gave her even a sliver of comfort was knowing that they would once and for all meet Oscar's new girl.

She laughed inside as she recalled watching Oscar's face upon this new revelation. She thought he was going to pass out, but he had finally agreed, stating that we must all come to dinner with an open mind.

"What's that supposed to mean?" Brianne had asked, but he had volunteered nothing more and they'd left Henry for a time to get some sleep.

Now, as Susan thought of her new task, she wondered if she'd be able to follow through with Henry's request. Maybe he wasn't thinking clearly. Perhaps he was feeling guilty that he hadn't been able to finish the case like he'd planned. Whatever the reason for his sudden interest, Susan had feelings of foreboding as she thought on presenting herself to Mr. Cardigan.

***

The place was boarded when she arrived, and everything was dark. Susan peeked inside one small window above the door which had been missed. Though it was mid-day the place looked even more uninhabited than it had that first day she and Brianne had visited. A sudden thought occurred to her that Fred had more than likely been brought in for questioning and that during the interview he'd had second thoughts about continuing with his business.

Susan peered out to the main street and watched the cars for a time, but she didn't see Fred. After a half an hour she turned and got inside her car and drove home, thoughts of Fred, who knows where, striking a strange chord within her brain.

The man was not only strange but inconsistent. While he had a terrific booth set up during the *Halloween Bazaar*, his own place was disheveled, and wasn't set up for the business. They'd caught him in a mess, with boxes and clothing and accessories strewn everywhere. It was almost as if he was searching for something, like a person would do when searching for Christmas decorations or camping gear – or a hidden lost shoe. It was almost as if he wasn't setting up shop at all!

In a moment's thought, Susan turned the car around. She needed to talk with Justine Commons.

The woman wore pink and smiled at her across the desk as she arrived. With a slight knock on the partially opened door, Susan walked in. As before, pelicans and pink struck her with great force. It was all she could do to sit down without staring at everything instead of the woman she'd come to see.

A hand reached out. "So, Susan, right? Come for more questions?"

"Yes." Susan sat.

Justine waited.

"What do you know about Fred Cardigan?"

"Who?" She adjusted her blouse.

"Fred. The owner of *Clothing to Die For*."

"Oh, he's in trouble, that man. Didn't you hear? Was in jail for questioning. Let him go. That girl, what's-her-name, was charged."

"Katrine…"

"I could hardly believe it when I heard. Imagine killing your sister."

"I don't think she did it."

It was the first time Susan had voiced her opinion to the public, but her opinion was a feeling really, coupled by the assignment her husband had given her to find out more about Fred.

"So…"

"I'm not really sure who did it, that's why I'm here. Fred, what do you know about him?"

"You mean besides what I read in the paper? Let's see. Well, this was the tenth year or so that he's set up a booth, though it was last-minute this time, but that probably doesn't matter. What may interest you is that he paid double. He applied after the deadline and I was going to use his spot for a sitting area. You know how tired folks get walking about. A nice bench or two, you know. But the man was insistent."

Susan blinked over at her. "Anything else?"

Justine pressed down her suit coat – sort of a purple-pink. "Well, let's see. Up-teenth year, paid double. Well, he really hit it off with Carly Petersen. This is her first year. I think that's all I know."

"Have you ever been inside *Clothing to Die For*?"

"You mean the one outside of the show? No, but I hear it's boarded up. They found that girl's shoe in the dumpster out back. I feel so sorry for her. I mean, getting jealous because you like the same boy, that's hardly a reason to kill someone you love."

"Where did you hear that?"

Justine was silent. She bit her lower lip. "Well, in the paper, of course. She reached inside the right-hand drawer and pulled it out. "I can't believe you haven't seen this."

Susan reached for the paper. It was dated the morning after her husband's operation. She skimmed the contents.

"But this is just an interview with you," she said.

"Of course."

"It's you that speaks of the jealousy between the sisters. There is nothing else here."

"Well, of course. Why else would one sister kill another except out of lust?"

"Lust?"

"Look, you came here for questions. I am trying to give you answers. Obviously, even though you're some sort of great detective, you missed reading this great article."

Susan's skin burned. "Anything else?" Susan asked.

"Well, there was this one thing."

Susan waited.

"He came here the other day. Said he was closing up shop. Told me he was leaving. I asked him where, he wouldn't tell me."

"Where's all of his inventory?"

"How am I supposed to know that?"

"I don't know." Susan thought of the love triangle that she didn't think anyone knew about besides herself and Henry. But the question remained. Where had Fred Cardigan put his entire inventory?

**

Brianne and Oscar were out for school break and Henry was home resting in front of the television set, and *directing traffic,* his exact words in regards to his children. That's how she'd left them.

She traveled alone, taking in the recent snow, the way the ice had grown crystals overnight on the wheels of her car, but it was at *Holiday Hours* that she'd done an honest-to-goodness double-take.

The door jingled, announcing her arrival.

Carly smiled over at her, forcing some sort of engagement.

"Hello," Susan offered. "I'm in need of some new Christmas ornaments." The aroma of sweet pine met her nostrils as she surveyed the room. But what was that in the corner?

The woman waved her hand to the back wall. "All of the ornaments are there. If you'll follow me, I'll show you the ones that just came in."

The sprightly 25-year-old directed her down one aisle to the back of the store. All Susan could think about – other than the clothing hanging in the far-left corner, was the woman's high heels and how even her hair bounced behind her as she walked. It reminded her of some sort of hair commercial.

"Now, these little jingles just arrived yesterday," she began, touching some silver and gold rendition of star light, star bright. "And these," she began, pointing to some red tasseled fireflies, "keep you thinking of summer even though it's almost Christmas."

Susan swallowed.

"So, when did you decide to offer clothing?" she asked.

"Oh, well, just for the holidays."

"How come?"

"We all need festive outfits don't we for parties and such?"

"Susan wanted to ask about, the *such*, but decided against it.

"Seen Fred lately?"

"Fred?"

"You know, the owner of *Clothing to Die For*?"

"Oh, well, actually, these are his clothes; I mean these are the clothes that were in his store. He just needed a little help." The woman was pale, and she was holding her hands awkwardly behind her back.

"So, where is he?"

"Fred? Oh, I don't know. I haven't seen him in days."

"So, when did he drop his inventory off?"

"The clothes? Oh, I don't know. That bit in the paper really disturbed him."

"What bit?"

"You know, that part about the shoe being found in his dumpster and all of the blood and that girl. It just made me sick."

"How did Fred feel?"

"Oh, he was terrified I can tell you. To have someone die in his booth and then find that shoe on his property, he just had to close the store for his own safety."

"How long have you known Fred?" she asked.

The paleness of the woman's face suddenly changed to red. "Why, I don't know. I guess it was at the *Halloween Bazaar*. Yes, that's when we met. At the *Bazaar*."

"You don't seem too sure of that."

"Well…I mean do you have any more questions?" The door jangled and she turned. "Another customer, will you excuse me?"

As Carly retreated to the front of the store, Susan made her way to the clothing section. Strumming her fingers through the sheer tops and tanks, she kept an eye on Carly and the customer who had just entered the store. The back room was just a few steps away, if she could just get to it without being noticed.

Another jangle of the door meant another customer, and as Carly turned to greet the man now entering, Susan slipped into the back room.

It was full of clothing and shoes and accessories. A few boxes lined the back and sides of the room; smaller boxes, more than likely with ornaments inside, were numbered and shelved down the center. It was all Susan could do to keep her hands from shaking and her heart from beating frantically inside her chest, but she continued through the aisles, checking an occasional box, for what, she did not know, until she came upon a pair of red stilettos. Like the ones used for the murder weapon, the heel was high enough and narrow enough to plunge into any unsuspecting head. But they were of a different style; Susan could see that right away. A slight movement made her stop. It was coming from the door through which she'd just entered. She stood still, wishing she had been looking through the clothing in just that moment, instead of the shoes – a much better hiding place.

In moments, the footsteps drew closer – heavy, breathing steps that did not sound like the steps of a woman.

She held her breath as the steps drew near, wishing she hadn't entered, wishing with everything she had that she had stayed up front.

She felt his breath on her even before she looked into his eyes.

"So, you have found me. Now what?" Fred asked.

"I, ah…"

He grabbed her by the wrist and slung her to his left. "This way," he ordered. Near the back door, he pushed her to the ground. "Now, you sit here. I have something to say, and when I say it, you'll never come back here. Never."

The strange man was wearing a blue bow tie and a Mr. Roger's sweater, just as before. He looked down at her with less than friendly eyes, however.

Susan tried to breathe calmly. She placed her arms across her chest and waited. The man paced. His heavy shoes spoke volumes about his injustices even before he spoke them.

"The police will never get me inside that police station again," he began, still pacing, still slamming his black patent shoes against the cement floor. "Even after all of the questions they asked – they demanded that I stay in town just in case they had further questions. I knew it would come to this, that girl with her shoes. I knew it."

"So, you sold Roxanne Anderson the shoes she was killed with?"

"Obviously. But the police knew that. They've had their eyes on me for months, and you snooping around didn't help any."

Susan held her breath.

"That girl changed her clothes in my dressing room…"

"So, the dress?"

"Mine. She didn't come to the show that way."

"What did she…"

"Shut up and let me talk! She came in some old sweats. Said she needed an outfit – quick. She spoke as if her life depended on it." Fred laughed hollowly and continued. "I hid the clothes for months. That night you came around snooping I'd finally managed to extricate them from the back room, only you didn't find them."

"Where are …"

"Shut up!" Fred stopped and peered down at her. "I know what you think. You think I killed that girl. That I set up her sister as the killer to get the police to search elsewhere. But I tell you I'm innocent!"

"So…so why am I back here? Why have you stopped me?"

"You were trespassing! And…you needed to know. I am tired, tired of running. Carly was the only one who would help me, the only one."

Susan was visibly trembling. Either this man was speaking the truth or he was crazy.

"Carly. You think we're romantically attached. If only that were so, but she has been my friend when no one else would."

"And the clothing? Was it ever really about the clothing?"

Fred's face paled. "What do you know about that?"

"I know you're hiding something. Not just the sweats, but something else. You've planted the murder on Roxy's sister, but something else is going on, I can smell it. Your shop was always a mess. And that day my daughter and I arrived, you were going through boxes, looking for something. What?"

"The shoe. I was looking for the shoe!" Suddenly, Susan could see that Fred's bottom lip was trembling. He was afraid. Of what? Of who? Her?

"I couldn't remember what box they were in. They were all stacked high in the main room before I brought them out. I'd closed the shop to do that stupid event. Someone called. I was here at the store, trying to get the clothing hung. They told me that if I didn't get rid of the evidence that I would be blamed. "Get rid of the shoe," she said. "Get rid of it or they will think it's you!"

"She?"

"It was a woman, but I'd never heard the voice before. I found them in a box just before you opened the door and walked in. I pushed the box to the back hoping you wouldn't notice. When you were gone, I dumped everything out back. I had to get rid of it. The next morning I felt safer than I had in months. The dumpster that held the shoe would shortly be picked up and I was looking forward to that. I watched the truck with hope as it carried away the evidence, feeling grateful that it was all over. But that afternoon, the police were at my door. There were a million questions, and then I was let go. Seems they'd found the killer – her sister."

"But her sister didn't do it."

"She's as crazy as a loon from what I hear. It was her sister's blood on that shoe."

"I know." Susan was still visibly shaking, but stood. She looked into the eyes of Fred.

"I want you out of here," he said. "You can tell the police what I've told you but I won't be returning to that place. This is my last night here. I will be leaving this and everyone..."

"What of Carly Petersen?"

"What of her?"

"You like her. You're in cahoots or something. Tell me."

"She is a friend. That's all. And she understands…"

"What does she understand?"

Fred was riveted to the spot. Even his shiny shoes were silent.

"It's up to you now. I hope you find the killer."

***

"You did all that shopping and didn't find anything?" Brianne asked, her hands on her hips. "Really, Mom!"

"I'm sorry. I found Fred."

"That old guy who owns the store?"

"Yes." Susan sat. "Where's your dad?"

"Back in bed. So, what did he say, this Fred guy? Did he admit to anything?"

Brianne turned from her to the refrigerator and pulled out an apple. She took a bite and sat down.

"He sold Roxy the shoes and the new dress."

Brianne took another bite. "Did you call the police?"

"No."

"Why not?"

"He told me he was not going to be there and that I was wasting my time."

"And you believed him?"

"Why wouldn't I? The man was crazy; I thought I was going to pass out in the back room. I got out of there and home as quickly as I could."

"Your face is flushed."

Susan looked down at her hands. They were still shaking.

"So, what else did you discover?" Brianne asked, taking another bite.

"Fred wants me to tell the police what I know."

"Sounds like he's really in league with that woman."

"Maybe. He says they're just good friends."

"Hmmm.

Oscar leaned his head in. He was standing in the hallway. "Secret talk?" he asked.

"No. You can come in."

"Good, I'm hungry." He reached for the refrigerator door and opened it.

"So, what's our next step?" Brianne asked.

"I need to tell the police what I know. They'll probably go over there anyway and question Carly, but I wanted to get my wits about me before I made it."

Brianne stood, and walking past her brother, dropped the core into the kitchen trashcan.

"I went out while you were gone, too. Seems this Johnny is as tight-lipped as a jar of pickles."

"Pickles!" Oscar gasped, reaching in.

Brianne returned to the table and sat down, licking her fingers. "I mean, he is one strange guy. One minute he is flirting with me as if I would even think of going out with him, the next he is walking away, screaming at me for lack of privacy. It was weird."

"So, you didn't learn anything."

"No, or, just one thing. But I'm not sure if it means anything. He told me about how girls were strange, how they were never as they appeared. He really seemed to have a thing for Roxanne, and her sister, Katrine, which didn't surprise me, though it did seem to embarrass him a bit. What would make Katrine the girl he liked over Roxanne, being as Roxanne was the solid sister. Follow?"

Susan nodded, opening and closing her hands. Finally, she relaxed a bit.

"He really liked Katrine better, but perhaps that makes more sense. They were both a bit extreme, Johnny with his hair and clothing styles, and Katrine with her emotional stuff. He didn't know she'd been seeing a counselor, and when I mentioned it, he smiled. When I asked him to explain why he preferred Katrine he didn't answer me. That's all I got."

"Maybe Katrine did kill her sister. It's an awful thing to think. Gads, I can hardly believe it. But, what if it's true? What if she goes into court and they find her guilty?"

Susan's heart stopped. Maybe she'd been wrong. Everything seemed to turn to Katrine, especially the shoe with her finger prints on it. Still, could the girl think clearly enough to plant the shoe in a dumpster, and not just any dumpster, but the dumpster behind Fred's place? Fred had said that he had the shoe and that a woman's call had forced him to finally rid himself of it. So, what was the truth?

What of Katrine's emotions? Counselors couldn't give any information about the clients they helped, so she'd be wasting her time going there. And the parents, they were so full of grief, what else could she possibly ask them?

"Brianne's right," Oscar said suddenly, taking his stash of food to the table. "That Johnny kid is a real creep. It didn't even matter that I was standing there. He treated me as if I was invisible or something. It was just nice to get out of there."

"You were pretty rude," Brianne said, her eyes following her brother as he chewed his first bite of sandwich. "It's a miracle I was able to get what I got."

"Just like a girl. I protected you and you can't even thank me."

"Protected me? I thought you two were going to get into a fight!"

"What?" Susan's thoughts turned.

"We weren't going to tell you." Oscar turned from the table, sandwich in hand. You worry about everything."

"Well, a fight is a big thing."

"Nothing happened." He took another bite. "Do we have any chips?"

"Top cupboard, right."

Oscar stood, walked to the cabinet, opened the door and grabbed the chips. He returned to the table, and opening the top, took a couple. "I mean, this guy would really never have fought me." Oscar flexed. "He doesn't have the guns."

Brianne rolled her eyes.

"Oscar made fun of his hair and the guy went ballistic."

"I didn't make fun, exactly. But I just don't get it. Once you're in college, I thought people slowed down a bit, started dressing more professional and stuff. The guy looked like a girl."

"And you told him that?"

"Not exactly. I just said he looked 'sweet'."

Brianne was trying not to smile.

"The guy shouted at me, called me a 'jock,' so I smiled back at him. That only made him angrier. He said I was a 'jerk,' and that I needed to keep my opinions to myself. I told him that he needed to keep his *hands* to himself. It was just a statement. I'd heard about all of the girls he was dating. I thought it would open him up to some…ah…discussion." Oscar took another bite of sandwich.

"Then Johnny swore at Oscar. Called him a wiener."

Susan tried to remain calm, though a smile was tweaking at her left cheek. She didn't really like Oscar's name either, but she hadn't given it to him, and he was her son now, and so she'd had to live with it. What else could she do?

"I had to get between them, Mom. I had to break up the fight. Johnny stormed off."

"Yeah, his hair bounced behind him as he walked away. He had it all brushed back and…"

"Okay, I get it." Susan stood. "I'd better go check on your dad. We'll talk later."

Walking down the hallway, Susan couldn't help but be struck by how easily her children could argue. Still, she was glad they'd both come home safely. Thoughts of Katrine killing her sister filled her mind once more, and as she entered the bedroom, she looked in the direction of her husband. He was still asleep.

News

Officer Crump squinted at her, his balding head reflecting off the overhead light. "How is your husband doing?" he asked.

"Fine."

"You should have called. The man's probably gone by now."

"I didn't worry."

"You should have." Crump typed something into his computer. "This makes him a suspect."

"I know, but he said he wouldn't be there if I sent anyone back."

"Perhaps, but you're also listening to a potential criminal."

So, she was stupid, would always be stupid when it came to sleuthing. Still, Fred had said he was taking off.

"And this woman, Carly Petersen, you spoke with her?"

"Like I said. They know each other, and I think it's more than just a brief meeting at the *Halloween Bazaar*. I get the feeling that they've known each other much longer than that."

"Ah – ha."

"They seem close. She was protecting him. Took in his entire inventory. Who would do that? I mean the entire inventory."

"Including the shoes?"

"Like I said. But the ones in the back were a different style."

"So, Fred Cardigan told you that he'd taken the shoe and the sweats?"

"Yes."

"And he'd hidden them?"

"In one of the boxes until the call came."

"A woman. Did he recognize the voice?"

"He said no, but I'm wondering…"

"Is there anything else you'd like to tell me?"

"I think Carly knows something."

"We've already spoken with Carly, but we'll do so again. Anything else?"

"I guess not."

"You said your husband was doing fine. Where is he today?"

"At home in bed."

"You're doing the detective work on your own then?"

"No," she lied. "He is able to get around some."

"Well, don't let him overdo it."

"I won't."

Officer Crump stood and reached out his hand. She shook it. His palm was clammy like a recently retrieved fish. She placed her hand in her pocket and turned.

"You hear me, Susan?"

She wasn't a child, but things would never change. "I hear you," she said, not turning.

***

Henry was sitting up. Though still weak, he was getting around more than he had at his release now some two weeks previous. Susan was more than glad; she was relieved that Henry was on the mend. But that didn't mean there weren't many pills to take and many visits to the hospital to be made to check on his condition. Currently, they were seeing Doctor Richards every week, and if things continued well, in two months the journeys to the hospital would be quite a bit less frequent.

Susan felt bad about lying to Officer Crump, but she also had to continue with the investigation even if it meant Henry consulted her while in bed or eating his afternoon meal. Besides, Brianne and Oscar were a big help, when they weren't fighting, and were managing to get in and speak with folks that wouldn't even turn an eye to her.

Among them, Mrs. Sadie Chartreuse, whose view of Susan was slim in praise to say the least.

But Brianne had worked wonders and had a glowing report as she returned the following Saturday with her brother.

"That girl can clean circles around a shark," she began. "And she can flirt at the same time."

Oscar blushed. "You didn't tell me she was a 'looker.'"

"Which reminds me...have you set up the day for us to meet your girl?"

Oscar shrugged. Not that again. "How about when it warms up a bit?"

"Sounds like you're stalling." Brianne blinked at him from the other side of the couch, leaning over to see his expression.

"Not...stalling. I thought we'd wait."

"How about we invite her for dinner next week?"

"How about we invite your mother?"

Susan clamped her mouth shut. She hoped she wouldn't see her mother any time soon, and it wouldn't fare well to have Oscar's new girlfriend here at the same time anyway.

"Well, at least you can tell us her name," Brianne asked, still leaning so she could see him. Susan sat back – she was in between them. It would be fun to see how this played out.

"You don't need to know that."

"Why not?"

"Because."

The tension in the room was thick. Susan had wondered for months why her son hadn't volunteered the information. It was past time.

"No. We need to know now. I'm going to make some cute dinner place cards."

"No, you're not."

Brianne giggled. "Yes I am. I'm going to make some cute ones and I need her first name, just her first name, so I can get started on them."

"I don't know. You're really going to make them?"

Brianne stood. She walked to her brother and sat on the edge of the chair he was sitting on. He peered up at her. "Really, Brianne, you can all wait."

"But what about Dad. What if..."

"Brianne!"

"Sorry Mom. It's just dumb that he won't tell us."

"Perhaps we should talk about what you learned from Sadie Chartreuse."

"Oh, that."

Brianne stood, and instead of returning to her spot on the couch, took a chair opposite her brother. "Gads, Oscar is such a doofus, but everything worked out anyway. Sadie was sweet. She went over everything we'd previously discussed with some added details."

Susan's ears prickled.

"You're not going to believe this. Sadie told us that there was more blood than what was near the paper towel dispenser. She remembered little droplets, kind of in a line from the toilet, but figured they must be from someone else – but the other day she was deep cleaning the bathroom, something she gets to about every other month – and there was a thick wad of paper towels in back of the toilet bowl near the floor. When she got on her knees to search it out, there was a note."

"Impossible."

"I'm serious."

"So, where's the note?"

"Sadie told me she showed it to Veronica for feedback and that the woman got really nervous. She pried it from her fingers before she'd gotten past the first line and flushed it. They were both working in the bathroom evidently."

"What did the note say?"

Sadie was pretty unclear about that. She seemed more worried about Veronica's reaction. But she did say the note was fairly short."

"Did she read any of it?"

Oscar was smirking now, leaning over towards her. "This is the unbelievable part," he began.

"Okay…"

"The note began, 'Dear Brianne… but that's all she was able to read before the note was yanked. I almost stopped breathing when she told me. I couldn't believe it. And then I was asking her about talking to the police, if she'd done that, and if not, why not. She confided in me that she hadn't. 'I'm afraid of cops,' she said."

Lame excuse, Susan thought but didn't say.

"What do you think it means?" Brianne asked, her eyes unblinking.

Susan wasn't sure. The girl had obviously needed to talk to Brianne about something; something that couldn't wait for a meeting at the Greenfield cafeteria on campus the next morning. She tried to recall the first note, now with police, something about being afraid for her life and about being watched. Roxy had known she was being followed so she'd slipped the note in a well-hidden place, hoping to find Brianne again where she'd first left her – and give her perhaps some brief words on where the note would be hidden. Perhaps she'd been attacked in the bathroom, and making her way to *Clothing to Die For*, had finally collapsed. Again, a nagging thought struck Susan's mind. Why was her daughter the chosen one in the first place? Why would Roxy choose her out of all of the people at the *Halloween Bazaar*? And then something else, so obvious, struck her. Why had Roxy called her daughter, *Friend*?

Susan's heart was pounding but she had to ask. The question had been asked before as they'd sat in the kitchen, as Brianne had revealed the first note seemingly a life-time ago. And she hadn't thought of it then, taking in her words about finding someone nice who might help her, someone like Brianne who smiled a lot and was friendly and connected with others easily.

"So, how did you know Roxanne?" she asked.

The Guest

"What?"

"Tell me, how did you know Roxy?"

"I... please, Mom, don't get mad."

"At what?"

"What I'm going to tell you."

Susan was still. It was as if the air could speak if she sat silently enough. As it was, her daughter was squirming in the chair, looking over at Oscar and back into her eyes. "Please, don't hate me."

"I could never hate you." Susan breathed in deeply. "You are my daughter. I love you."

Small tears slid from Brianne's eyes. "I... a while ago I went to this party. It was the first party I'd ever been to." She paled. "Months ago, before the *Halloween Bazaar*, Roxanne and I talked. It was only one time, Mom. After she was killed I didn't go back to another party. I couldn't until that night. You were asleep." She looked over at Oscar. "We..."

"We went to a party," Oscar ended. "I was with her so don't worry."

"Don't worry? Did you drink?"

Brianne sat still, her lips parted as if she wanted to speak but couldn't.

"I did. I wouldn't let Brianne."

"Oh, Mom, I snuck one! Just one! It...it made me sick so I didn't have another."

"Beer?"

"I...I don't know. It was nasty."

Oscar shrugged. "I didn't know. Really, Mom." His eyes blinked in her direction. As usual, Henry wasn't in the room, was never in the room. She didn't know what she'd expected to hear, but it wasn't this.

"So, you met Roxanne Anderson at a party, is that what you're trying to tell me?"

"Yes." The words were spoken together, as if even their words were suddenly in league with the deception.

"I can't believe it."

"We're sorry." Brianne was at her feet. "I know I'm not old enough. Oscar brought me home early. I told him I was feeling sick."

"Though I didn't know it was over the booze."

"How could you keep this from me? From – from your father?"

"Dad was easy," Brianne quipped. "We just needed to sneak out without you hearing us. We caught a ride from one of Oscar's friends."

"Who?"

"The girl you now won't be inviting to dinner."

Oscar smiled, but Susan could see it was forced. Brianne was still pale, and Susan wondered what could possibly happen next. Raising children was not a walk in the park; it wasn't even a walk to work, but something else entirely.

***

She'd spoken to Henry the night previous and they'd come up with a plan. They were all seated at the kitchen table, she and Henry on both sides, and their children at the center. Outside, the weather was white and cold. Susan was happy to be inside, though the coldness yet remained in her heart.

"So, what do you think we should do about this?" Henry asked. He was looking better today, but Susan could see the weariness underneath his eyes. He winked over at her.

"And you, what do you have to say?" asked Henry, looking at Oscar. He'd promised Susan that he would take this seriously. That he wouldn't smile even once, though he was known to have taken a few sips at their age – at least at Oscar's age.

"We won't do it again," Oscar said, placing his elbows on the table and glaring over at his sister. "Will we?"

"No, we won't."

110

"Is that so?"

Susan was silent. This she'd promised Henry as well. Her words often got the best of her.

"Yes!"

"Well, that's good. So, Brianne, why do you think your mother and I are angry?"

"Gads."

"Well?"

"I don't know. I guess because I snuck out and drank one beer and got sick and I didn't tell you that I knew Roxanne."

***

It was morning, and the breakfast hadn't yet been fixed.

"You can ground me if you want," said Brianne, glaring at her brother.

"And you?"

"I was drinking before you knew me."

Silence.

"How long have you been drinking?" Susan asked.

A glare from Henry prompted her to issue a sorry.

"Well?"

"Since I was 10. It was easy. Father."

"How often?"

"At parties, mostly."

"And your sister?"

Oscar stared out the window. "She caught me once, in the back yard. After that, I promised I'd take her to a party if she kept quiet."

"Skipping school?"

"No."

"Cutting class?"

"No."

"How often have you snuck out?"

"Just twice – that is, the both of us."

"When?"

Brianne blanched. "The first you already know about. The other was just the other night."

111

"Whose party?"

"I..."

"Whose party?!"

"Matty's."

"Matty Slack's?" Now Susan was in an uproar. She couldn't remain silent. They'd have to tack her mouth shut.

"Yes."

"Gads, Mom! I told him you'd find out, and that you'd scream at us. Why do you think we wanted to keep silent?"

"Now, don't go blaming me for your indiscretions!"

"But you get so upset! All the time!"

"No I don't!"

"Yes, you do!"

"Yes, you do, Mom."

"Honey..."

"Don't tell me you're not upset." Frankly, Henry didn't look anything but pleased. He was actually smiling at her. "Come on, Honey. Let's talk this out. We have good kids."

"Kids who lie and drink! And I told you not to smile!"

Henry laughed as she stared at him, her eyes like hot kettles. How could he be so relaxed at a time like this? Didn't he feel...anything? Why were they all laughing? She must be the biggest joke on the planet, no, the universe.

"What – What?" she squeaked, sounding more like her daughter than herself. And then it came, she couldn't help it. It started with the laughter and then the tears, and then her side, oh, her side!

"Happy Valentine's Day!" Brianne sang, though Valentine's Day wasn't for another week.

***

After she'd finished preparing the dinner – the casserole sat in the oven baking, they'd all talked, and it seemed to Susan, for the first time in a long time they'd really – talked. In the end, Susan was sure why Roxy had confided in her daughter, and she was happy to finally have things out in the open, at least in her and Oscar's regard.

Though Oscar hadn't known that Roxy had confided in his sister at the party, Brianne had been worried about it ever since. Every time her name came up, after every visit, after every clue. And now, for the first time, she could speak openly about her deception.

But the words that had been spoken into the evening, words about Roxanne worried that she was being followed, about her sister treating her rudely, about the games that they all played at her expense. As for Oscar's girlfriend, he still had not told them her name; not even Brianne knew of her secret identity, but after the consent was given and the call made, Susan had dropped her interrogation, and Henry, he'd smiled at her from across the table, pleased that she'd been able to let this one go. After all it was only a day, and well – Susan had a sneaking suspicion she knew who it was anyway.

Near 6 p.m. there was a knock at the door. Susan's heart started but she didn't get up. She sat on the couch, her face to the door, Henry at her side. Brianne sat on the floor nearby, staring at the door.

A burst of cold air filled the space in the kitchen and drifted to the room where they were sitting. And then she was there. Miss Matty Slack.

Her blonde hair was pulled tightly into a ponytail, and as she released herself from her thick gray coat with a furry hood, Susan stood. Of course, who else? She obviously wasn't dating Johnny Reimbolt anymore, and maybe that was okay, though Susan wasn't so sure. The girl was beautiful, anyone could see that, and she carried herself with poise well beyond her years.

Susan looked over at Oscar briefly, but he wasn't looking her way.

"So, Matty, are you ready for dinner?" she asked.

The girl blinked, blushed and handed her coat to Oscar, who was still staring at her as if he couldn't believe she was there. But maybe she wasn't. Maybe this whole thing was a dream, or some strange nightmare that would continue with secrets she didn't know, and guests she'd somehow expected.

Questions Answered

The casserole, a tossed green salad, and dinner rolls filled the plates. Her mother hadn't been invited, Susan wasn't even sure what she was doing tonight; no call had been made at either end, and this was probably good.

Most of the conversation concerned the case anyway, and it wasn't long before Susan and the others realized why the girl, Matty, had taken a hiatus from college.

"I hate to gossip, but I was afraid of Johnny. He was so good to me at first, and then things changed. He wanted to control everything I did."

"So where did you go?" Susan took a bite of salad, hoping Matty would reveal the answer.

"Home. My grandparents live in Alaska."

"That's your home?"

"Well, it was for a time, Brianne. My parents were going through a nasty divorce and I stayed with the grandparents for a few months. When I returned home, my parents were no longer together, and it no longer felt like home."

Brianne nodded. "I know what you mean. Living here is my first home."

"I figured. Oscar tells me that your other parents were not very good to you."

"Pretty much."

Matty blinked and took a bite of casserole. "This is really good. Thanks for inviting me."

Susan wondered where Matty's parents were. There was something almost ethereal about Matty, and Susan tried to remember the first impression she'd had of her at the college as she'd directed the students in the ways of the campus. She'd seemed assured then, much more assured than now, and it almost appeared to Susan that the experience with Johnny had softened her, made her more reflective and aware, or her son had had some effect on her. She wondered how long the two had been dating, but from what she could deduce, Oscar had been dating Matty all along – even before Johnny had come into the picture.

"I hope you don't mind, but I need to let you know that Johnny dated and probably still dates lots of girls, including Katrine. In fact, I think they were still dating up until her arrest."

"Do you know that for sure?" Susan's fork was posed in mid-air, a noodle dropping to her plate as she spoke.

"Pretty sure. That girl is a real nut case. Sorry, but they make a great couple if you want to know the truth."

"Didn't Johnny also date Roxy?"

"Yes. But the truth is he's always liked Katrine better. I guess it's because they have so much in common."

"Like what?" Susan took a bite, trying not to lean into the table too eagerly for an answer.

"Oh, dancing mostly. He took us all dancing, but it was Katrine who really got into it. She had all of these secret dates with Johnny before her sister found out. She was pretty mad, I can tell you. And I'm sorry Katrine is in jail. She might be a little strange but I don't think she did it – killed her sister I mean. Sorry," she added softly. "I know you and your husband have been trying to find the killer, and I want you to know I'm here to help."

"Thank you." Susan took another bite of casserole and the conversation turned to other things. Namely, how she and Oscar had met – at a party – months ago, and how they'd stayed in touch through the weeks through emails and phone calls.

"I really wanted to tell you who I was talking to," Oscar interrupted as they were clearing the dishes and preparing for dessert, "but Matty asked me not to. She wanted to stay in hiding for just a little bit longer. After orientation, things started heating up. She didn't want to speak to the cops and she didn't want to run into Johnny."

"So, how long have you two been dating?"

Oscar paled. "We've just started dating. We were friends before that."

Matty blinked. "We were good friends for a long time, but when Johnny and I began dating, well, I still needed someone to talk to. Johnny didn't know. Well, at least not at first. It was none of his business anyway."

"So, does he know you're back?" she asked.

There was a pause. "He didn't until the other night. I've been squeamish ever since."

"Don't worry," Henry said. "Have you talked to the police about your suspicions?"

"Not yet. But I think I'm ready now."

***

After Susan learned that Katrine had pled not-guilty to the charge of premeditated murder, she also learned that the girl's trial would be held in sixty days. That meant she had less than two months to find the real killer and bring her to justice.

Based on the words of Fred Cardigan, it had to be a woman, the same woman who'd called him with the warning to get rid of the shoe and sweats. But how had she known he had them? And why would he have them? Better to leave the shoe alone. It just didn't make sense that he had the shoe if he wasn't the killer. It didn't make sense that Katrine's bloody fingerprints were on the shoe, did it? Unless he was protecting Katrine, and she really was the killer. But why would an old man do that? Why would he take the shoe, hide it, along with Roxy's outfit, unless he was mixed up in this murder somehow?

Thoughts like these rambled in Susan's mind as she tried to sort them out.

The only reason Fred would have the murder weapon, the shoe, was if he was the murderer.

The only reason Katrine was labeled the murderer was because her fingerprints were on the shoe.

And then there was this strange Johnny Reimbolt. Somehow, he was mixed up in this. Somehow. Could he have killed Roxy because of something, some fight, some threat? Passion was a huge thing and Susan wouldn't put it past him to kill for some love triangle. But if he was the killer why weren't his fingerprints on the shoe?

Susan slept little that night. The new year was fast approaching, and she had to open her eyes to a clean slate. The following morning, she cleaned up the entire Christmas affair and prepared for the day. Her thoughts turned to Jane Dove whom she'd neglected to visit. She had a small gift for her; almost a token, and felt the need to take the gift over. She almost felt sorry that she'd not taken the opportunity to see the children or to help with the needs of *Honesty House*, but it had been all she could do to get through Christmas with her own family and provide for their needs. She suddenly felt selfish, and then she remembered that Henry had been in the hospital too. She could only do so much.

Jane was happy to see her. "I thought you'd dropped off the face of the earth!" she said first. Then taking her by the hand she led her friend into the waiting area. It was a great place to sit, not only because of the added space – Jane had had some extra funds to spruce up the place with some new paint and furniture – but because, after all, the space was for visitors, and Susan was feeling like a visitor here. She was grateful Jane could take on the responsibility. She had taken more and more on as Henry had gotten sicker. Though Susan had made a few phone calls, the past month had been far too sparse in visits. Susan couldn't remember having even visited once.

"So, how is Henry?" she asked next. They both sat, children around them playing or laughing. No one turned in her direction.

"Fine, fine. Henry is up and around but the doctors expect six months for total recuperation. He can't even drive yet."

"How long does he have to wait?"

"Six weeks. You should see the scar."

Jane lifted her eyebrows. "I think not. So, when can he return to work?"

"I'm sorry. You must be overloaded. And I didn't even come for Christmas."

"That's okay. We had fun. So many people donated gifts; we even had a visit from Santa Claus. But I'm in need of a break if you want to know the truth."

Susan thought briefly of the hired help, but remained silent. If there was a problem with them, Jane would say something.

"Henry has at least another month before he can return, maybe two or three."

"Oh."

"I'm sorry. I'll come in more if that will help you. The kids will be back in school come January, and I can fill in where you need me."

"That would be great. Are you sure?"

Susan nodded. "You're doing a great job here; I only wish I could give you *Honesty House* for good, instead of one of us making new decisions all of the time on who should own it."

"Me too, actually." Jane looked away for an instant, and then her eyes turned back to Susan's. "I mean, I hate to be a pain, but things are getting more expensive by the minute, and though the donations come in fairly frequently, sometimes I've had to take the money out of my own pocket."

"Jane!"

"I'm sorry. Really. But these kids need so much. They almost feel like my kids."

Susan remembered feeling the same way – once, before her own children had come to live with her. But Jane had never married, and she didn't have any children. Susan wasn't even sure if she had time to date.

"I know." She reached out her hands and Jane took them. "You are a fine mother to these kids."

"Do you really think so?"

"I know so. Here." She reached inside her purse and pulled out the small gift wrapped in shiny red paper. A small tag read: 'To the best friend I've ever had.'

"You didn't have to."

"I wanted to."

"I have something for you as well." Jane stood, walked a few steps to the front desk and then reached over and behind it. She produced another box about the same size. This one was wrapped in silvery gold paper. A small bow was taped to the top. "Open it," she said.

"You first," Susan prodded.

"Oh, okay." The process was slow as every piece of tape was removed and the lid opened. A piece of batting concealed the gift and was quickly removed. Looking inside, Jane gasped. "A locket! How did you know?"

Actually, Susan didn't. She'd searched and searched for the perfect gift, only to come upon this one quite by accident. But it had spoken to her in some strange way. Susan had purchased it, brought it home, and scrounged for just the right picture to place inside. Once placed, she'd wrapped the gift and slid it under the Christmas tree.

Jane opened the small window and looked inside. "Oh, it's you!" she sang. "How thoughtful! Now, even when you're not here, you'll be next to my heart."

The gesture was sweeter than anything Susan could have said. Tears welled in her eyes. As she brushed them from her cheeks, Jane clasped the chain around her neck. The necklace fell just below her collar bone. She touched it softly. "What a thoughtful gift," she said. "Now, open yours."

Susan slid off the silky bow, tore the paper from the box, and gingerly opened the lid. Hers as well had a piece of batting. Susan picked it off and placed it on the table. It was also a necklace – no, two necklaces – that joined together to make one heart.

"One is for me, the other is for you. Now, whenever we're apart, we can remember our friendship."

The gift was almost too much for Susan to take in. Evidently, they'd both been on similar wavelengths as the gifts had been chosen, and it occurred to Susan that her friend was missing her just as much. She pulled the two chains from the box. "What side do you want?"

"Your choice."

Jane would always be her right-hand woman so she handed her the right side of the heart. "I know it might sound silly, like we're in grade school or something, but these are 14 karats."

Susan laughed. "Really?" She wrapped her side of the heart around her neck, touching it briefly with her fingertips.

"I walked up and down that silly boutique until I thought I'd go crazy. And then, there it was. The woman was so nice. She makes these herself, you know."

"You mean you bought this for me way back in October?"

"You sound as if it was a year ago. Yes, I have to start my shopping early. It's the only way I can get everything done."

Susan thought of her last-minute gift and remained quiet. "So, when did you get it? We were together the entire time at that bazaar."

"Oh, you know, I have my ways. You were sort of preoccupied with finding your daughter. I'd seen the necklace earlier and had asked the woman to hold it for me. When all of the commotion was going on with the girl and all, I snuck over to her booth and bought it."

"You didn't want to see what had happened?"

"I saw enough. Besides, the wounds were still fresh."

"What – sorry, I didn't think of that."

"That's okay." Jane smiled over at her. "Well, I'd better get back to work."

Susan blinked, realizing for the first time how loud the room had become. And wasn't that a fight between two boys in the corner? "Where is everyone when you need them?" Jane said, standing. She embraced Susan briefly. "Just a sec."

Susan stood and watched her friend. In moments both boys were hugging each other and Jane was returning to her. "Don't worry about me. I can make it for a week more. What day can you come in?"

"School starts on the second."

"What time?"

"Eight or so."

Jane smiled. "I can hardly wait," she said, embracing Susan one last time and returning to the boys who had not surprisingly started another argument.

***

Henry was making lunch, his red hair combed like the entrails of a fish. A sudden chuckle reached her lips as she shut the door, waves of snow flowing inside.

"So, you're back. And just in time."

"What are you cooking?" She set down her purse.

"Grilled cheese."

"With all of the leftover turkey in the fridge?"

Henry laughed. He reached for her with his left hand and gave her a little squeeze. "I'm bored out of my gourd with turkey and lying on the bed. Well, mostly." He winked at her although they hadn't made love in weeks. But there were plenty of other things to do – they cuddled mostly.

Susan reached her own arm around his waist. "Then make two," she said.

"I was planning on it. How is Jane?"

"Oh, as loving and stressed out as possible."

The bread sizzled in the pan as Henry turned it to brown the other side. "That's my fault. You know, even when I was there I really wasn't there. My detective work was almost more than I could do. Thanks for helping out."

"It was nothing."

Henry placed the sandwich on a paper plate. "Here, you can have the first one. I'll make my own."

She reached around him for the plate.

"You can let go," he said.

"I kind of like standing here."

He squeezed her tightly. "Me, too."

"Where are the kids?"

"Where else? Matty has invited them over."

"Both of them?"

"Now, don't worry. We have to trust our kids sometime. They said no more drinking, remember? I thought it was pretty sweet. What college student wants to hang out with a 15-year-old?"

"Well, she is pretty sweet."

"I can't get to the bread."

Susan moved from his side, reached again for her plate, and headed to the table. She sat. Henry had already placed two sodas on the table.

"If you're wondering, I figured you'd be at *Honesty House* about an hour or so. And I figured if you didn't show up, I could eat the second sandwich as well as drink the soda."

"You did not."

"I did." He turned to her briefly, then back to the stove to turn the second sandwich. Susan took a bite of her own.

"It's good."

"But of course." In minutes, his own sandwich finished, Henry sat next to her at the table. "I am so ready to get out of here," he said, touching his chest. "We need some time away."

Susan nodded, though the time away was more than likely something he needed.

"After the new year, let's take off."

"I have a better idea. How about New Year's Eve? We can stay overnight at one of those ritzy hotels. Go to dinner. Pretty much lay around. We don't even have to stay awake for the count down."

"You always hated that anyway."

He took a bite and smiled over at her. "Well, what do you think?"

"I think I'd be worried. What if Matty is having another one of her parties?"

"I already asked her. She said no. She'll be at her mother's."

Susan gaped at him. "So, you've already decided on this adventure?"

"Right. Want to come along?"

***

After a myriad of promises by her children, she and Henry were off. Henry had had a visit with the doctor, and as long as he didn't drive, short distances were fine.

But Susan wasn't so sure. What if the bed was too hard or something? What if he couldn't sleep? What if he got too anxious and wanted to make love?

Henry had only laughed at her concerns, though his solemn attitude had returned once she'd asked the doctor how long they had to wait. Six to eight weeks seemed like a lifetime to Henry, but he was still sore from the incision and still a little worried about breaking it open anyway. He was already on an exercise program and the doctor suggested short walks on their overnight vacation together.

Still, Susan worried about his lack of energy, and was anxious herself about Henry returning to normal in all facets of life. He still slept a lot, still did little before he felt tired, and was still quiet about many of his feelings. She tried to spend as much time as possible with him and when the day arrived to make their trip, she felt calmer about getting away than even a week ago.

It had been three weeks since the operation and this time away was well needed.

As she watched Henry sleep on his side of the hotel bed, she would read or write a note, or watch television. Sometimes she would sit at the desk at the window and check her email. When Henry was awake, they'd discuss politics, their children, and the case. And they stuck with the doctor's plan on all accounts.

Upon returning the next afternoon, the house was in full swing. Brianne was winning her brother at Wii Sports, and the two of them had

122

hauled soda, chips and cookies into the living room for their fiesta. The room smelled of sweet sugar and a mixture of food that more than likely shouldn't be mixed.

"Hey, you're home already?" Brianne bounded from the couch. It was Oscar's turn to try and swing the tide in his favor. He barely looked at them. "Hi," he said.

"Dad needs a nap so can you turn the sound down?"

Oscar paused the game and reached for the button on the remote. "Did you two have fun?" he asked, and then blushed suddenly.

Brianne smiled. "You didn't play tennis or anything, did you?"

Henry chuckled. "Nope, but it looks like you two are."

"Just bowling. Oscar sucks."

"What?"

"Sucks. Sucks. Sucks."

Oscar flexed his muscles. They rippled slightly under his shirt. "Maybe this is a good time to stop," he said, setting down the remote. Before you go to bed, Dad, that is."

"Oh, that's right. We had a visitor last night."

"Not Matty, I hope."

Oscar grinned. "Sorry, but no. It was your mother. She was pretty peeved."

"About what?"

"You didn't tell her about Dad."

"You didn't tell your mother?" Henry asked, sitting down on the couch.

"I didn't. I couldn't. I just couldn't."

"Wow, Mom, you're sure afraid of her."

"I'm not afraid." She looked over at Brianne. "I just…"

"You're afraid." Oscar sat on a chair opposite, followed by his sister. "I know you don't like her but she had every right to know."

"Why, so that she could harp on me for something else? Ever since William's incarceration, she's hated me. I just couldn't do it."

"Gads, Mom, you sound just like Matty."

"What?"

"Like Matty. Last night she said she was angry at her mother. Angry at her dad. She can't forgive either one of them, and so she sulks about it all of the time."

"I thought you didn't see Matty last night."

"I – we didn't." Oscar placed his hands on his lap; coiled his fingers around each other. "Okay, so I saw Matty last night. I might as well tell you, you'll find out anyway."

"But it wasn't his fault. Really, Mom! After grandma left in a huff, Matty came over, and she was upset. Her mother had canceled her trip to Alaska at the last possible moment, but that's not why she was crying. We waited for her to tell us but all she could do was cry. After a while we offered her a soda. She wouldn't take that either. She just cried until finally Oscar gave her a hug and told her he was there for her. She quieted after that but said she was in danger. Johnny had come over unannounced. Her dad was at work. She'd opened the door without even thinking about it and he'd pushed himself in. Mom, she had bruises all over her face and neck. We told her to go to the police, but she told us she was too afraid. What if Johnny came back? What if he hurt her again?"

"Where is she now?" Henry asked, his own hands curled into balls in front of him.

"Home. She wouldn't listen to us. It was pretty late when she left, but she wouldn't listen to us. Gads, I was so scared, but Oscar was calm."

"Not inside I wasn't. I tried calling her today. No answer. I called the police station. She hasn't been there. About a half an hour ago, she called me, said everything was fine now and not to worry. I told Brianne we needed to keep busy so we wouldn't think about it. That's why we're playing this stupid game. We told you we wouldn't leave the house and we didn't, even when we wanted to."

"I appreciate that."

"Oh, Mom it was so scary! I didn't know what to do!" Brianne wailed.

"Well, it sounds like you did the right thing," said Henry, standing now, and walking slowly into the kitchen. "I'll call the police."

***

A day later, the kids were back at school and she was back at *Honesty House*, though much had been discussed at the dinner table the afternoon prior – among them Johnny and his temper, what was currently happening with Katrine Anderson, and what more might be learned in talking with those who had worked at the *Halloween Bazaar*. And then, of course, there were those who cleaned the facility, and Justine Commons, event coordinator at *True and Vine*. Unfortunately, Fred Cardigan hadn't, as yet, reared his stranger-than-fiction, head. He was still gone somewhere, and Carly Petersen – Fred's assistant of sorts, had been as straightforward with the police as a squirrel on a hot day.

In the end, assignments had been given. Henry was to call the Anderson's for a sort of *checkup*, Susan was to make her rounds once again with the cleaners Cecil and Little Miss Sunshine, Veronica Edwards; she hadn't yet talked with Mark, and Brianne and Oscar would make another visit to campus and ask around at Greenfield cafeteria. It was, after all, the place where Roxy had told Brianne to meet her. Perhaps this was more than a 'waiting' place, but a place with answers.

The day went smoothly enough at *Honesty House*, and it seemed to Brianne that Jane looked more relaxed than a week previous – she even laughed some and confided to Susan that she'd begun to date again. His name was Charley, and she'd looked him up online to see if he had any 'history' before taking that first step.

Where had they met?

At *Honesty House*. He'd brought a boy in – not his own – who was alone in the streets. The boy looked to be about five. Jane had researched and researched and finally the answer had come and the parents had been found. The boy had gotten lost and had been living in the park underneath the freeway for at least a week.

After that, it was like Charley found strays all over the place – including dogs, which Jane told him quite frankly was something she couldn't help him with. He'd asked her if she cared to go out. When she told him no, he found other ways to come and visit – he needed an address, his mother was sick and what should he do, his car needed towing. After about two weeks Jane had relented. Though the excuses to see her were bad, it was obvious he had a kind heart.

At least she hoped so.

Some things would take longer to heal than others.

This Susan knew for sure. Henry was going on his fourth week of rehabilitation, and the doctors were hopeful that he was improving; still, things were slow-going at home, and Susan continued to take on work that Henry typically did himself.

It was on her fifth day working with Jane that she finally had the time and energy to seek out Mark – the very part-time employee working at Inglewood. As she expected with the curt answer from Sadie, Mark was working the ticket booth out front. Once a year Inglewood serviced a grand movie night for families – and this was the weekend. He was busy too, as family after family, their noisy children complaining of the cold as they waited in line, waited to pay their entrance fee. But $5 for an entire family was a great price, and even Susan had to admit that if she'd had young children she might just have been doing the same thing.

As it was, she was freezing, hoping for a break in the line so she could speak with him. He seemed a fine enough boy, probably a sophomore or junior in high school, though he might have been a senior. He was fairly short, about 5'3" or so. Still, as she approached, and he asked her for her money, she noticed a slight growth of beard on his otherwise tanned face. His hair was blonde, and his features, striking. Bright green eyes lit up his face, and when he smiled a large dimple creased his left cheek.

"I need to speak with you about the death of Roxanne Anderson," she began.

"Who?"

"Roxanne, the college girl who was murdered here in October."

The boy blanched. "I didn't know her," he said.

"Can we meet later? When do you take a break?"

"About eight, when the movie starts."

Susan reached for her cell phone and pushed a button. "That's about an hour from now. Would that be okay?"

"I guess, if you want, but…"

"Hey, lady, we want to get inside, too."

Susan turned back. A woman with at least four kids stood behind her. They were pulling on her shirt and one was crying mercilessly within her arms."

"Sorry. I…"

She turned back to Mark. "Let's meet over there." She pointed to the west side of the building where she knew there was a second entrance.

"That door is locked during stuff like this. I'll find you. Where will you be?"

"In my car. It's parked, there, by the curb."

He reached his neck forward.

"Come on lady!"

"The blue one?"

"Yes."

"By the white one?"

"Yes."

"Okay, I'll meet you there after my shift, though if you're not inside it when the police come around, you'll probably get a ticket. That's a no parking zone."

Susan turned. Her car seemed fine for the time being, but as she approached, a paper was tacked underneath one of windshield wipers. She pulled it out and got inside.

At five after the hour, Mark approached. He knocked on the window. Evidently, she'd fallen asleep. The windows were as steamy as a sauna, and she rubbed her eyes as she opened the door. "I suppose I'm safe in here," he said. "You must be an undercover cop."

"Actually no, but I do work for a detective agency." She showed him the card she'd designed at her husband's prodding. They all had one now, including Brianne.

He looked down. "Okay, so what do you want to know?"

"Is there a place we can talk inside?"

He shook his head. "Not really, the movie is blasting and the kids are yelling. Last year, I tried to block out the noise and get some sane time by going inside one of the offices and shutting the door, but it didn't work. I still heard the screaming."

"Okay, then, I'll make this short."

"Sounds good."

"So, you said you didn't know Roxanne."

"No, but I heard enough about her after the fact as if I did know her. Everyone talked about her for days like she was a celebrity or something. I heard she looked like one."

"But you didn't know her."

"No, like I said…"

"So, what kinds of things did your co-workers talk about? Did any of them appear to know her?"

"No. Well, maybe. Sadie had this thing. Oh, I don't know. She was always saying even after the girl was dead and buried, "Do you think she's prettier than I am, and stuff like that. I would always say, 'Of course not. I don't even know her. Besides, she's dead and in the ground by now. Worms are…'"

"I get it. Did she ask you anything else?"

"Asked me on a date once, but she's like five years older than I am."

"That must have been pretty complimentary."

"I guess, but I really don't like Sadie. Yeah, she's beautiful and all, but – don't tell anyone I said this – she's a control freak. She thinks she's the boss of everything."

"But she is your boss."

"Yeah, but she just hits you in the face with it, you know. I was cleaning up after a fall activity once – hate those urinals – and she told me I was doing it wrong; as if she's ever peed in one."

Susan swallowed. "What did you say?"

"I told her to bug off. I said, 'Well, at least I'm not cleaning up blood like you always have to do in the girls' bathrooms.'"

"How did you…"

"I've been in charge of special events – cleaning up that is – even though some of the stuff I do isn't in the job description."

"Oh, anything else?"

He turned to her fogged window, and began to write something in it. "See this?" he asked after he was finished.

Susan leaned to the right. The word *stiletto* was printed on the window, only it was spelled: s-t-i-l-e-t-o, missing one of the t's. '

"Stiletto?" Susan whispered, not really trusting her voice.

"Yeah, strange, huh? I mean, I saw this word on a piece of paperwork, the one she carries on the clipboard to check our work, to see if it's satisfactory, as she puts it. The funny thing is I'd never seen a word like that on her paperwork before: only stuff like slacker and needs improvement and stuff like that. The word was sort of written to the side of the job chart."

"When did you see it?"

"Oh, I don't know exactly, but it was before the girl was found dead, I know that for sure."

"Anything else?"

"She was funny every time someone brought up Roxy's name. I was all for that weird guy that works for the clothing store; Cecil said he thought it was Sadie. When Sadie heard the gossip she yelled at all of us. After that, I didn't dare ask her about the word, though after a few days I went in search of the paper. I figured if I could find it written down, that the paper would be some sort of proof I could give to the police. I couldn't find it and I searched everywhere. As it was, I didn't figure the police would believe me."

"Why not?"

Mark smeared the word on the window with his fingers. "I'm a kid."

Inglewood

Sadie was furious. "You have what?"

"A warrant." Officer Crump stood next to Susan, and Susan stood next to Henry whose body was tilting slightly to the right. Today wasn't one of his best days but he wouldn't have missed it, he told Susan, for the world.

It had taken almost two weeks to get the warrant. They were heavily into January by then, and the frost outside was as thick as the lying words that now creased Sadie's beautiful lips.

"I haven't done anything wrong. Why would you need a warrant?"

"There is reason to suppose you have in your possession, a piece of evidence."

"Evidence, for what?"

"Roxanne Anderson's murder." He handed Sadie the warrant.

"Unbelievable! You think I killed that girl. Impossible! I didn't even know her."

"We need to look anyway. You can stay here, or remand yourself to the hall if you'd like."

They were in the bare room that served as Sadie's office. There was a desk, a chair and papers stacked on the table. Also, hooks on the wall with nothing on them.

"I hope we've done the right thing," Susan said.

"Why?" offered Crump.

"I don't know. It's just a feeling."

It took less than half an hour to scour the room, but when nothing was found other than the typical fare for supervising a bunch of cleaners, Officer Crump took Susan aside. "You did say she owned a clipboard. I don't see one here. Maybe it's time to ask her."

He turned to the door.

"Wait!" Susan raced to him, placing her hand against the door's opening. "You don't really think she's going to hand over evidence, do you?"

Officer Crump looked at her wearily. "We should have asked about it outright. She probably doesn't even remember writing the word down. It was probably an afterthought or something."

Susan sighed. "I don't believe it. I don't believe you. She's not going to openly give you that clipboard. A fight will have to come first."

"Susan." Henry was standing behind her, his hands against his back as if he was propping himself up. "Listen to the officer. He knows what he is doing."

Susan tried to breathe slowly. She stepped away from the door.

"Miss…Miss Chartreuse. Can we have a word?"

"Surely, Officer."

Hands on hips, she could see them speaking back and forth. Susan turned to Henry. "I wish I could hear them."

"Maybe it's good that you don't. We'll know what this is all about momentarily." She felt an arm around her waist. "See, they're already finished."

Sadie blinked at her wickedly as they walked by the desk. "This clipboard?" she asked, raising it above her head.

Where had that come from? She'd checked the desk herself. And then she noticed the silver tape. "I suppose I can tell you that I have to hide this thing all the time. People here are always changing things if you know what I mean."

Susan breathed in and out slowly. There, in the woman's hand was the clipboard, and on the clipboard, was the very paper in question, it just had to be. Sadie handed the clipboard to the officer.

"As you can see, most of my employees do a fair job. Veronica Edwards for one, she always does what she's told. Cecil does very little damage that I can ever complain about, though Cecilia, not to get them confused, and how could one anyway? I have to send her back for re-do's all of the time. And Mark? He hates instruction of any kind. High school student. Any questions?"

"Yes," said the officer. "Is this your most current chart?"

"This chart is for January – see the date? I have a chart for every month of the year." She closed her lips suddenly, almost pursing them.

"Where do you keep the others?"

"I don't."

"Surely, you keep records of…"

"Now, tell me Officer, ah Crump, why I would want to keep records of such slovenliness."

"Slovenliness. Now that's a fine word, but I have a serious question. Why don't you keep the old records? They would be good to compare. See and monitor progress."

"You're right of course. Maybe I do have them at home or somewhere. Yes, they're probably at home. Anything else?"

"We'll need to see those records."

Sadie brushed her fine hair from her eyes. "And why would that be, Officer? They are just records. I have allowed this, ah, detective here and her daughter to search this place, to check the bathrooms and anything else I can think of to help them in this case. A girl has been murdered, why wouldn't I want to help out…"

"Yes, why wouldn't you?" Officer Crump was not to be put off. He stood, hands in his pockets, holding his ground.

"Well, I guess I could show you. Why do you need to see them? They are just boring notes about equally boring people."

"In any case, I would like to see them. Would you like to bring say, the last six months' worth with you to the station, or should I swing by here tomorrow?"

"It's Sunday; my day off."

"Well then, Monday."

"I can do that. Is that all?"

The officer nodded. Susan was just dying to speak but decided against it. What could she possibly do anyway? Sadie wouldn't have the records for the officer's view until Monday anyway, and she'd just have to wait.

***

"You can't go."

"Why not?"

"This is police business, that's why."

"But I want to be a part of the stake out. I want to see her leaving her home with the records. I want to see her get caught."

"It will just be Officer Crump and myself sitting in a car. Nothing exciting."

"You've got to be kidding."

"Honey, please. He's taking me along but it's only because…"

"You're a detective and I'm not."

"I just don't want you to get hurt."

"And what about you? You're in no condition to do a stake out!"

"I'm fine."

"No, you're not!"

Susan was visibly shaking. Just today, some six weeks into her husband's recovery, Dr. Richards had pronounced that he was improving but still needed to be careful. Walking was good, and getting out, but not too much and absolutely no strenuous activity. What if he had to jump out of the car and chase that woman? He wasn't even supposed to be back to work for at least another one-and-a-half months!

"Susan, you've got to understand. I have to do something. I can't just sit and sleep and eat anymore. I'm bored out of my goard."

"Please, let me come along!"

"Susan."

"Henry, please! I could never forgive myself if something happened to you. Please!"

In the end, the far end, Henry had called Office Crump, and he'd relented. The woman had no past issues to be reckoned with. No jail time. No crime. She was probably as safe as her mother. Susan might have spoken up then but she hadn't. After the yelling match with her children, her mother hadn't called, she hadn't re-visited, and she hadn't sent a letter of apology. And maybe it was just as well. Still, Susan hadn't told the kids, only offering that she and their dad were going on a late-night date. Brianne had looked at her quizzically, too quizzically to make Susan comfortable, and Oscar had only shrugged his shoulders. "Okay," he'd said, turning down the hall to go to bed.

***

The heater was off and it was cold, colder than Susan could remember it ever being in her entire lifetime. Officer Crump would turn it off and on in spurts so as not to be detected. It occurred to Susan, sitting in the cold car, with the windows rolled up and the snow dancing across the windows that Sadie wouldn't have to leave her house to destroy the document. All she needed was a match and somewhere to burn the paper. But then she couldn't help re-thinking her initial thought. She would have to produce a paper after all, and could she forge one to look like the original? She'd seen the condition of the one currently in use, dog eared, and curled at the corners, a spill near the top. No, Sadie would have to use another tactic if she indeed was mixed up in all of this and if Mark had been right about the word written across the sheet.

She would have to leave her home. Sneak out never to be seen of again. The night was so chill, and fat snowflakes easing their way to lay still and lifeless on the windshield almost made it impossible to see out. But then, what was that?

"Be quiet, now," the officer said, hushing her.

Someone was leaving the house. Sadie lived alone, according to police records, and she was leaving alone. "Wait…wait."

"It looks like a suitcase."

"Shhh!"

"Where would she be going late at night? Look, is she putting it in her trunk? Why did she leave the house lights on?"

"It's a good thing," offered Crump. "We can see everything."

"Aren't you going to go – "

Suddenly, the door opened and the officer stepped out. Susan breathed a sigh of relief when Henry remained in his seat. In moments, she could see the officer leading Sadie back into the house. The door was shut. "I promised him ten minutes," Henry said. "After that time, I'm going in."

"When did you promise?"

"Guilt usually produces flight."

"Can you turn on the heater?"

"I suppose it wouldn't hurt – now," said Henry, sliding to the driver's side and turning the engine over.

Susan sat up straight, the adrenaline in her veins increasing. "Just don't drive!"

Henry chuckled softly. "Don't worry, I won't."

Nearly ten minutes later, the front door opened and Officer Crump walked down the driveway to the street where they were parked. Clicking open the door he stepped inside. He had a bundle of papers in his hand. "Just as I thought," he said.

***

She'd tried to hide it with marker, the pen lines of the word, Stiletto, revealing the truth. But even Susan could see the telling word.

But what did it mean, really? How involved was Sadie Chartreuse in the murder of Roxanne Anderson? It didn't take long to find out.

The questioning began the next morning. Sadie had volunteered her services freely, or so it seemed when Henry told her she'd be meeting with Officer Crump. Two days later the information filtered through the officer to his friend, and then from her husband to her: Sure, she had written the word down, only after the killing, only after the police had questioned her and she wanted to remember the murder weapon if she came upon it. No, she had no connection to Fred Cardigan, other than she knew he was a vendor. No, she didn't know the victim, didn't know her sister, Katrine. Did she also know Carly Petersen? Yes, but only because she was also a vendor.

Why had she been so evasive about showing them the word on the clipboard? Why, she didn't want to be implicated, wasn't that obvious? She knew who had spoken up, that Mark Rand. He was always stirring up trouble. Sure, it made her nervous talking about the dead girl, trying to locate the murderer. Weren't she and her fellow companions there to do their jobs?

Susan sighed. Of course, she would say that.

Why did she try to leave, suitcase in hand?

She was scared. Wouldn't you be?

Susan walked to the fridge, grabbed a soda and sat down on a kitchen chair.

"I can't believe it. I just can't."

"It would have been nice for her to confess something – of course," Henry began, "but we still have all of this scattered information, and nothing is connecting. Until the information connects, we have little to nothing."

"And what about Fred. Has anyone seen him?"

"No one."

"What did Roxanne's parents say when you called them?"

"I told you."

Susan couldn't remember hearing any conversation about the Andersons. "Tell me again."

"They were still grieving and thanked me for their call. Katrine is hanging in there; going through some tough times."

"I can imagine."

"Drugs are nothing to write home about."

"Drugs. You didn't tell me that."

"I'm sure I did. Besides, what does it matter?"

Susan's heart seemed to stop. She touched Henry's hand. "Are you feeling okay?"

He nodded, but she wasn't so sure. She would have remembered if he'd told her about someone's drug problem. She would have remembered that.

***

"Mrs. Anderson?"

"Yes?"

Henry was at work in the home office. She was on her phone in the kitchen, at least for now. The kids were at school and wouldn't be home for a few hours. The time was now.

"This is Susan James. How are you?"

"Fine, fine. But your husband already called."

"I know. I just wanted to ask you something."

"Alright."

"How long has your daughter had a drug problem?"

The line was silent, and Susan wondered for a moment if the woman had hung up or if the call had dropped. Finally, the words came. "As I told your husband, going through drug withdrawal is a hefty thing, especially on top of the murder charge."

"I know and I'm sorry you are going through this."

"Why do you need to know how long my daughter has been on drugs?"

"To find the real killer."

"What real killer?"

"I don't believe it's your daughter, and I don't believe you believe that either."

"I don't know... I... What I mean to say is. My girl might have done it. She was on drugs, more than likely at the time of the murder. Her counselor couldn't say anything about that, but once in jail I was told that she'd been tested. I didn't want anyone to know." A large sob filtered through Susan's phone.

"I realize that people can do things while on drugs that they normally wouldn't do, but that doesn't mean that your daughter killed Roxanne. I don't even think with her emotional problems that she could have done that."

"But what about her fingerprints? The blood? There is so much evidence against her."

"And don't you find that intriguing, Mrs. Anderson? So much evidence against a girl who has never struck out at anyone in her life."

"That's right. She wouldn't hurt a fly."

"And if not a fly, then not her sister."

"My daughter says she's been on drugs, pills mostly, for a few months. She tells me college was hard and she was having trouble with Johnny, and lying to her sister about that didn't help." She paused, as if trying once again to take it all in. "If it wasn't her, then who do you think it was?"

"I have my guesses but nothing is firm yet. Do you know where she purchased the drugs?"

"The police are working on that. Seems she bought them on the street for the most part. But I really shouldn't be talking to you about this, should I? I'm not paying you anymore."

"I know, but Henry and I just wouldn't feel right if we didn't follow this through."

There was a slight pause. "Then it wouldn't be right for me not to continue with the payments. I'll send one off tomorrow. And Susan?"

"Yes?"

"Thank you for understanding. The neighbors, well, that's another story."

"How is your son?"

"Funny you should ask. Not well. I may be taking him in to see a counselor."

"I'm sorry, Susan. I really thought I'd told you."

Susan paced the living room. The children were home and it was time for another meeting. "Knowing that Katrine was on drugs opens up some things. I think I'm finally able to connect some of the dots."

"Which ones?" Brianne asked, her eyes wide.

Henry sat silently on the couch with Oscar who was trying to keep his eyes open. He'd had another date with Matty and had stayed out far too late. Now it was Saturday morning and all he'd wanted to do was sleep in.

"What if she's been set up?"

"Well, you've believed that all along," said Henry.

"I know, I know. It's just…with the drugs, the girl is not only set up; she's easily set up.

"What do you mean, Mom?"

"Consider this scenario. Someone like Fred Cardigan kills Roxanne because she's going to share what she knows with the police – that he's secretly selling drugs to teens and college students, for example. He kills Roxanne so she doesn't open her mouth and get him in jail. Because he is selling drugs to Roxanne's sister, Katrine, he feels he can easily pin the blame on her. This girl does not think straight, she is in counseling, and he's heard from Katrine's own lips that her sister has the boyfriend she wants. The day of the *Halloween Bazaar*, Roxanne comes to his booth. He has been trying to find a way to rid himself of the worry that she presents, but he doesn't know Roxanne personally so this is difficult. When she comes into his booth that day looking for a new dress and shoes, he gets an idea. The girl will be meeting her boyfriend in a few minutes, she says, and she wants to look nice. Can he get rid of the old sweats? This is almost too easy, thinks Mr. Rogers."

"Who?"

"Fred Cardigan, Brianne."

"Why do you call him Mr. Rogers…"

"Shut up. I want to hear this." Oscar is suddenly awake. He is leaning forward, taking in every word. The tiredness is gone.

"All Fred needs is a weapon, but he doesn't have one. And then he thinks of the shoes. The shoes would do it. They have a small, thin heel and would make a great puncture wound. Only he can't leave his booth. He'll have to get someone to do the dirty work for him."

"Who, who?"

"I wondered about that all night. Who could Fred get? Well, it would more than likely be a woman, and don't you think, the same woman who called him and demanded he get rid of the shoe?"

"So, who was it?" Henry asked, fairly intrigued now. "Who could old Fred get that would cater to his whims?"

"Someone who was deep into drugs, his drugs, that's who."

"Well, then he could have gotten Katrine to do it from what you've said."

"True, but he could have also gotten someone else, anyone who had a bone to pick with Roxanne."

"Not Matty!"

"Probably not. I've gotten to know her some since our first meeting at the college. I don't think she could have done it."

Oscar breathed a visible sign of relief. "Then who?"

"Remember Cecilia? She works at Inglewood and she's a past girlfriend of Johnny's."

"Boy, that's really stretching it." Henry again. He was poised on the couch, his fingers intertwined. Susan wondered if he was getting too anxious. But she had to continue.

"Let's just say that Cecilia is instructed to kill Roxanne. They know each other. We already know she feels as if Johnny is boyfriend to every girl on the planet. I saw her rage that day that your dad and I talked with her, or rather, listened as she vented her frustrations with her many-timing boyfriend. She doesn't like Katrine either, and would have been pleased to make both of them miserable. Fred promises her drugs without pay, for life. He promises her the moon if she will do this one thing for him. But he doesn't have much time. Roxanne will be gone soon, meeting up with Johnny. He'll have to move quickly and so he gets in touch with Cecilia, tells her that her boyfriend is back with Roxanne, and promises her many quick fixes ahead if she does this one thing for him."

"This sounds almost too good to be true. Really Susan."

"Wait!" Susan was stubborn if nothing else.

"Let me share this last part. Everything fits snuggly after the killer makes her move.

Unfortunately, Roxanne feels as if she is being watched, and she passes Brianne that note. What she doesn't realize, at least at first, is that she might not have tomorrow to speak with her. She races into the bathroom and writes up another quick note, hiding it in an inconspicuous place. She has plans to find Brianne again and whisper where the note is, only Cecilia has followed her and a fight ensues in the bathroom. Somehow Cecilia gets the shoe from Roxanne's foot. Either Roxy trips or is pushed or something and now the murder weapon can be used. It only takes one strike of the head, Cecilia is so angry. She has done her duty. Roxanne falls to the ground. As instructed, she takes the murder weapon with a piece of paper towel."

"What?"

"Just hear me out, Henry. She returns to Fred, hiding it somehow as she comes to him. He is waiting for the shoe's return and tells her to take it out of the building along with the sweats he's already slipped into a bag or something. Roxanne arrives moments later, stumbling to her death. As she falls, the piece of paper towel holding in the blood at her head falls to the ground. Fred picks it up, quickly. To everyone's eyes, the girl was stabbed here, and the murderer has run away with the murder weapon. There is so much commotion, so much shouting and screaming, that no one notices Cecilia escaping with the evidence. The police check Fred's booth and find nothing. His job is complete."

"Wow, Mom, what a story."

"You've got that right." Henry was smiling.

"What?"

"So, tell me how Sadie fits in. Why the word on the paper? Why is she so afraid? Why does she leave her home, or try to, in the middle of the night? And most of all, why would some old guy really care about murdering a drug client, if in fact, she was a client?"

"Like I said, she was going to expose him."

"Roxanne is a college student; not much pressure there."

"I know, but she's very articulate from what I've heard. Everyone liked her."

"Almost."

"Well, I think it's plausible, don't you Brianne?"

"Sure. It sure beats some of the movies I watch!"

"Exactly!" Henry frowned. "Besides, how are you going to prove any of this? Fred can't be found, though the police have been searching for him for weeks. Brianne already has a ton of evidence against her, and wait – the prints, Katrine's fingerprints are on that shoe, not Cecilia's. If anyone killed Roxy at that event, it was Katrine."

"Okay, detective, if Katrine killed her sister, why would she dump the shoe at Fred's? Why not anywhere else? The lake? The dumpster closer to her house? She could have cut it up into little, shiny pieces and hung it on her Christmas tree. Why Fred's place? And why would Fred lie and say that he'd received a call from a woman to put the shoe in the dumpster if that really didn't happen?"

"Wow, Mom."

"Well?"

"I don't know. Maybe she was high when she did it. Maybe she wasn't thinking straight. Maybe she wanted to blame someone other than herself, not thinking that there might be fingerprints – hers, on the shoe that she'd dropped at *Clothing to Die For*."

Messed Up

Susan's brain had congealed. It was Jell-O, or worse, dried glue. Henry was right. She'd just discovered a motive for Katrine not Cecilia. If she shared this with the police, it would just be more evidence against the girl whose family was trying to release her.

Maybe – no, definitely – she was too close to the case. Just days from now Katrine would go into court, and with the evidence already against her, she'd be sent to prison. Susan didn't even want to think about that – a young girl spending the rest of her life behind bars. But there was nothing she could do. The killer could also be Veronica for all she knew, or Mark or Cecil or anyone. All they needed was a motive, and from the list, Katrine had the strongest.

Because Katrine was mixed up in drugs; she might have been persuaded to do it. She loved and hated her sister, had every reason to kill her; her sister was vying for the same man. It was stupid that she could have thought it was anyone else.

The bottom line was that Susan had been duped, so wanting Katrine to be innocent. Why? Because her parents had already lost one daughter? Because now, with the imprisonment of yet another, they would be losing two?

She knew what it meant, not to lose children surely, but never to really have them. And she couldn't let that happen.

But what if it was true?

Tears graced her cheeks and she couldn't speak to anyone, not Brianne, not Oscar, and not Henry. Thoughts of her friend filled her mind, but she couldn't return today, could she? She'd woken up with a headache and couldn't be comforted.

But she'd made a list:
1. Cecil, the man
2. Kent, the Andersons' son
3. Matty Slack
4. Johnny Reimbolt
5. Carly Petersen

***

Cecil was hammering Sadie's work desk when she spotted him. It looked as if one of the legs was loose.

"Hi!" she said from the doorway.

Cecil looked up. "What are you doing in here?" he asked. Susan jangled the key in front of her. Mark Rand was her new confidant and he'd easily handed her the key, with these words of caution: Just don't let Sadie catch you. Of course, she won't be in for another couple of hours.

The boy was a big help, though a bit scattered if Susan was being honest. Still, he was a teen, hated his job, and hated Sadie even more. He would be thrilled if she proved she was the killer. Why had the woman written down the word 'stiletto?' and what had Cecil really seen that day when the man's hand had reached out for the paper towel?

"Do you have a minute?"

Susan placed the key in her pocket and sat on one of the folding chairs. Cecil grabbed a chair from the corner and took a seat opposite. "So, what do you need now? Still trying to work on that lame killing?"

"Yes –"

"I don't know what else I can possibly tell you."

"You said a man grabbed that paper towel as it dropped to the ground. How did you know that?"

"Are you kidding? Most women don't have hair on their arms like that. Besides, the man was wearing a silver watch, men's style. His nails were cut short, not polished in red. A man, like I said."

"Was the skin light or dark?"

"Light."

"And the hairs on the arm?"

"Seriously?"

Susan nodded.

143

"Dark I suppose. But it was really the watch that got me."

"Why?"

"The band was broken. It was attached with something to hold it together. Maybe a couple of those bread ties that you see or wires from a paperclip."

"But you said the man grabbed it. How could you see it that quick?"

"I was standing pretty close. I smelled the blood. The man's hand sort of shook as he crumpled the wad of paper towel and shoved it in his pocket."

"You didn't tell me that before."

"I thought I had."

"Are you sure the man put the paper towel in his pocket?"

"As sure as I'm sitting here. Is that all?"

"Not quite." Susan took a deep breath and plunged in. "If you were that close to the man, why didn't you see his face?"

Cecil hesitated. "Well, I suppose it had to do with the clothing rack that separated us. The movement was so quick, too, and then the man was gone."

"So, he must have been a fairly short man."

"I guess."

"And a fairly thin man."

"I don't know."

"Consider clothing hung on a rack. The clothing doesn't typically face the buyer, does it, but it hangs vertically. All you see is the side until you pull the item out and look at it, right?"

"I hadn't thought of that. Well, maybe the clothing was bunched together."

"Another question. Tell me why you were there in the first place."

"At *Clothing to Die For*? I ah, have to walk the area during the day, check for shoplifters and such."

"I didn't know you had those duties."

"Sadie is a sly one. She is always adding stuff to the list. The vendors, they're supposed to take turns watching for shoplifting, you know, walking the premises, but many of them have no desire to do it. They'd rather pay the extra money to hire me out."

"I didn't know that. Did Fred Cardigan or Carly Petersen take a turn?"

"I'm not sure. Justine would know for sure. She has to keep track of all of that –"

"– Wait – you know, I do remember something. Fred was there at his booth. I know that for sure. He – hated taking a turn and preferred paying the extra $20. But Carly, she wasn't at her booth that I remember. I heard from the gossip around here that she was flirting with Fred right before the kid screamed, but I don't remember seeing her in her booth after that."

"She could have been in the crowd. Most people can't avoid being a part of something exciting like that." She thought of Jane Dove in that second, who'd gone over to the jewelry lady to buy her Christmas present, but thought better of sharing the information. Besides, most people liked to be a part of something thrilling but not everyone evidently. Not Jane and not the woman who'd sold her friend the necklace.

"Do you know the vendor at the jewelry booth?"

"What jewelry booth?"

Susan remembered at least five of them that day. "Well, the booth would have been located near the place where Roxanne fell."

"The only one I can think of is called the *Jewelry Dive*. Miss Gretchen Conner is the owner. She's a nice older lady. You don't think she did it, do you?"

"No, of course not. But you did say the man who reached out for the paper towels was wearing a watch that you thought needed fixing."

"Yes." The man went pale. "You don't think Fred did it, do you? I mean the man is a bit squirrely."

Susan tried not to smile. *More than that*, she thought but didn't say.

"You know, come to think of it, the man who reached out could have been Fred. He's not way tall for a man and he's pretty thin, almost as thin as that bow tie he is always wearing. And there was a little boy nearby; did I tell you about him? He was screaming like a banshee."

"I remember hearing about him earlier in the case – from you – but nothing ever came of it."

"It's probably nothing, just some child who saw everything happen."

Susan's heart stopped. "What did the little boy look like?"

"I don't know. Only saw the back of his head. His hair was black."

Susan wiped her moist hands against her jeans. She'd already taken off her coat and it was draping over the backside of the chair.

"Anything else?" Cecil asked.

145

"Yes. You were fixing the desk when I came in. What was wrong with it?"

"Oh, just a loose table leg. If Sadie Chartreuse is anything, it's detail oriented. She hates anything out of place."

***

Kent smiled easily as he opened the door.

"Hi. Are your parents here?" she asked.

"Just Mom. Dad's at work."

"Why aren't you in school?"

"Mom has decided to home school me." He opened the door wider. "You can come and sit in here. I'll get Mom."

It was the first time she'd been allowed into the small room just off the front door; and with good reason – almost everything reeked of crisp white freshness. She sat on the couch and looked over at the 5x7 photo sitting on the dark walnut end table. It was of the two sisters, smiling, holding each other in a friendly waist hug. They were twins, almost identical, but not quite. Katrine's face was a bit fuller than Roxy's, and her eyes sadder, her clothing less put together than her sister's.

She looked up. "So, what have we to talk about today?" May asked, her eyes sadder and more distracted than Susan had ever seen them.

"I won't keep you too long. Actually, I have some questions to ask your son if that's okay."

"Kenny? Why?"

"It's just a feeling I have. How close were he and his sisters?"

"Well, he was fairly close to Roxanne before she headed off to college. They talked some."

"And Katrine?"

"With her it was mostly a hit and miss deal. One day they'd be speaking, the next they were angry at each other. But it never got bad, more like the silent treatment between the two. I think Katrine was a bit bothered that her brother was always hanging around, that she had little to no privacy."

"And after Katrine was sent home from school?"

"Things were different. They didn't speak to one another, didn't yell at each other, but neither did they talk. But Katrine was in a slump then. She'd eat all day until she got that job at the grocery store, and everyone seemed to like her there. She took off some nights and the next morning the two would be sitting in the kitchen not speaking."

"That's strange."

"Maybe. But you have to know Katrine. By then, the therapy sessions were thick, and I guess the drug use, though we didn't know it at the time, was almost daily. Maybe Kenny noticed something."

"That's what I wanted to ask him about. Have you talked to Kent much about his sister's death and the situation with Katrine?"

"A little, but he's only eight. I hate to scare him even more than he's been scared. Are you sure you need to speak with him?"

"I promise I'll be gentle."

"Alright. He's probably back in his room."

But he wasn't. In that moment, Kent stepped out from around the corner. "I heard what you said and I got to tell you something."

Hair rose up on Susan's arms. She beckoned him to come closer. As he stood next to her, Mrs. Anderson was quiet. "I hate Katrine. She was always doing stuff she wasn't supposed to."

"Like what?"

"Lying and taking things."

"What things?"

"Store stuff. And then sometimes she'd act funny and would yell at me. Roxanne wasn't like that. She loved me."

"How do you know?"

"She would take me places."

May nodded. "That girl was amazing. She didn't get as hung up with Kenny tagging along; actually, I think she liked being with her brother."

"What places did you visit?" Susan asked.

The boy looked up at her, blinking his large, dark eyes, the color of chocolate. "The park. The store. Cool places to buy things."

"What did she buy for you?"

"I don't know."

"Well, she must have bought you something wonderful if you're telling me about it."

"I can't. I promised Katrine."

Susan's heart thundered inside her chest. It was amazing, that all of these months later, she was finally asking someone who might actually know something about the murder. And it was Roxanne's brother no less. Still, he was very young and she'd promised his mother she would be careful. Susan looked at her now and the woman looked stunned, almost frozen, as she listened. Hadn't she and her son spoken about anything?

"I don't think she would mind if you told us now. You remember where she is."

"In jail." The boy sniffed.

"Yes. And she would want you to share with me anything that might help her. I think she would be okay with you breaking your promise."

"Do you really think so?"

"If you know something, Kenny, you must tell the detective." May was sitting stiffly in her chair.

"Okay. That day my sister died, I was there too."

Susan looked to May. She was as white as a sheet. "May?"

"I – I didn't know, I thought he was with a friend."

"I was. My friend didn't show up after you left. Roxanne was nice. She told me she was going to this cool Halloween place that I might like."

"She took you to the *Halloween Bazaar*?"

The boy nodded.

"No one told me you were there."

"That's because of the secret."

It was easy to see that the boy was scared. He was gripping his little hands together and looking down at the floor.

"What was it?"

"When I tell it, you can't get mad."

"We won't." Susan looked in the direction of May. A tear had escaped her eye.

"I was there with Roxanne, but I didn't know Katrine was. I didn't think she liked stuff like that. It was fun, too. I got to see some cool Halloween costumes."

The boy hesitated and Susan waited.

"I was looking at them and Roxanne told me to keep looking, that she would be right back. But she didn't come back and I got scared."

"Why would your sister leave you there all alone? She's responsible. Unlike…"

"It was just for a minute. I saw her walking up to someone. I could see her the whole time. She gave this girl something. She was here at the house."

"That's Brianne, my daughter."

"I was scared when I saw her."

"Why?"

"I thought she'd tell on me. Roxanne came back, but just for a minute. She said she had to do something. There was this lady. She made stuff. She told me to stay with her."

"Gretchen Conner? Was that her name?"

"I don't know. She was old."

"Then what happened?"

"I stayed with her for a long time while she made stuff and talked to people, but after a while Roxy didn't come back. I decided to look for her."

"You know better than that!" May stood, reaching for her son. "Why didn't you tell me?"

The boy looked at the floor as his mother stared down at him. "Because you would have been mad."

"You're darn right!"

"Perhaps you should sit. Let's see what else we can learn," Susan prodded.

May breathed heavily, released her son, and sat where she'd been before. Kent looked up at her, tears filling his eyes. "I walked around. I got lost. I was so scared, and then I saw her. I could see her above the hanging stuff. She was standing funny. I ran over. I ran…"

"What did you see?"

"She…she fell! She fell! I didn't do anything, I promise!"

He hugged Susan's leg. "I didn't hurt my sister!"

The wailing continued, the tears wetting Susan's jeans, until it was all she could do to remain silent and wait, stroking the boy's back. The cries were pitiful – a high pitched wail. May didn't move.

"I…didn't kill my sister!"

The boy shivered and then was suddenly silent as he looked back at her.

"There was a hand. It went over my mouth. Someone took me away. In this dark place, I realized it was my sister – Katrine had come to get me." His bottom lip trembled. "She said, 'You will not say anything, you hear? Promise me. You will not tell anyone!'"

May stood and walked over to her son. "Come here," she said, taking the boy in her arms and holding him closely.

"Anything else?" Susan asked.

The boy shook his head.

***

Brianne was quiet and so was Henry. Oscar was on another date with Matty. The three without him sat together on the couch, almost touching, their thoughts separate but joined.

"So, it looks like Katrine did it after all."

"I don't know, Brianne." She looked to her husband on her left. "It appears so…"

"The boy's testimony might not stand up in court," Henry said, looking into her eyes.

"Based on what I saw today, the child wouldn't make it in a court proceeding."

"The good news is that there are ways to get the testimony that are less frightening, and maybe the court will choose another option," Henry offered.

"Like what?"

"Perhaps remote testimony."

"What's that?" Brianne asked, leaning around her mother so she could see her father's face. Henry looked good today.

"They use another room at the courthouse, or somewhere close by, and hook up a CCTV. The child answers the questions but away from the heaviness of a courtroom setting."

"What do you think Katrine would think about that?"

"Not sure. The police tell me she's not been very forthcoming about anything. The girl has been going through some pretty extreme hallucinations. Getting her body free of cocaine has been an uphill battle."

Brianne squirmed uneasily next to Susan. "I didn't know she was on *that* drug," she said.

"You'd better believe it."

"And her parents didn't know?"

"Obviously not. Though they do now."

"Oh."

"I spoke with Cecil. When he reminded me of the scream of a child right at the time that Roxanne fell, I was reminded of the cry of her brother as

150

he explained the secret he'd been holding since October. The poor, little guy."

"Gads, so what happens now?"

"It's time to speak with Matty Slack."

***

As she fixed breakfast for herself and Henry, Susan pondered over the revelation of yesterday – both of them – but primarily the words of the boy. She wondered if he was okay, though the thought occurred to her that perhaps finally opening up would be the beginning of his healing. He'd been struggling; maybe there would be less of a struggle for him now that the secret was no longer a secret.

She felt disappointment for Katrine, more so than she'd felt the moment she'd first heard, and wondered how she could have asked her brother to remain silent about something so important. And yet, if she was the killer, she would do anything to remain anonymous.

Henry had already contacted the police department; his appointment was at 10.

Susan scooped the scrambled eggs onto the dish, adding a slice of toast and a pancake. If only she could go with him. His eyes twinkled as she approached.

"So, you're trying to fatten me up," he said, leaning his head down and taking a whiff. "I didn't think you cooked this stuff anymore."

"You need your strength."

"But scrambled eggs?"

"I know, I know. No jokes, okay?"

"Okay. But can I have a cup of sugar with that?"

She laughed.

"Or, are you not sharing your sugar anymore?"

If last night was any indication of Henry's progress, she was definitely sharing a bit more sugar.

"What are your plans?" he asked, taking a bite.

"I was hoping Oscar would take me over to Matty's house this morning."

"Why?"

"It's just a feeling more than anything." She dished up her own plate. "I mean, the girl has been really good to Oscar and vice versa. They appear to make a good couple…"

"But?"

"Oh, I don't know. Does anything ever seem to be too good to be true for you?"

"You mean, like our love?"

She nudged him playfully, setting her plate down and reaching for the pitcher of orange juice already on the table. Pouring herself a glass, she asked, "She hasn't had the best life with her parents."

"Well, neither did our kids before they came to live with us."

"I know."

"So, what are you getting at?"

She sat.

"I just think it's strange that our son has connected with her at all. He's younger than she is, and didn't she say they'd met at a party?"

"Yes. So?"

"Maybe I'm just up in the night, but I worry about Oscar. He's going to be attending college soon, and I don't want him to be attached."

"Are you telling me that you want to meet with Matty on his account? Does this have to do with the investigation at all?"

"Sort of."

"Now we're getting somewhere."

"I'm sorry. Sure, she might have some insights on Roxanne and Katrine, but if not, I may be able to weasel out some things about Oscar. See her intentions."

"See how serious she is about him?"

Susan nodded and took a bite. The eggs, they weren't half bad.

***

"Oh, hi Mrs. James. Come in. My dad isn't here. He's at work."

Susan stepped inside. The décor was a mix of unpacked boxes and furniture without pillows.

"Thank you, but I came to see you."

"We can sit over here."

152

Susan walked over to the beige couch. A slight tear graced one corner. She sat, feeling the springs underneath.

"Sorry. My dad hasn't gotten anything new since…"

"That's okay." She waved her hand. "I just wanted to check up on you."

Matty blushed. Today her hair wasn't pulled back and it fell straight against her shoulders. "I hope you're not worried about me and Oscar. He – he's nice and everything, but I don't have any plans of settling down if you know what I mean."

Susan smiled. One down and she didn't even need to ask.

"Actually, I came to speak with you about Roxanne Anderson."

"Roxy? Why?"

"You knew her?"

"Everyone knew Roxy. She was one of those girls who got around." The girl blushed. "No, I don't mean like that. She was just friendly. She could talk to you about anything, and usually would. I was sad when she was killed."

"Do you think her sister, did it?"

Matty blinked. "Everyone does. I mean, isn't all of the evidence pointing to her? She's sort of crazy, and with her sister on drugs…"

"You mean, Roxanne?"

"Oh, sorry, Katrine."

Susan was startled, but only for a moment. "Was Roxanne taking drugs?"

"Oh, gosh, I'm not supposed to say anything. I'm not. Okay, so Katrine is in jail now and can no longer hold anything against me. I guess I should have told you, all of you that night at dinner, but oh, I'm so sorry. There was this thing about Katrine… she'd learn something about you and hold it to your head like a gun. So sorry…"

"That's okay." If Susan could have reached for a pillow she would have. She was suddenly feeling sick to her stomach. Now what? Things were coming to a head in this case faster than she could keep track of them.

"You know I met your son at one of my parties. He was always so nice to me. We sort of clicked. He understood about Johnny and told me he would never hurt me like that. Johnny was a controlling creep, everyone said so, but he could be so charming at first. I fell in love with him instantly the moment we met."

Susan couldn't believe it. Was she swooning over him even now?

"When I found out about the sisters I was livid. That day we met, I already had my suspicions, but, oddly enough, you were one of my connections to finding out the truth about Johnny. He had those two sisters wrapped around his finger. They'd do anything for him. Even after the cat fights between them at some of the parties we attended, they'd still want to be with him, and they fought like that to the bitter end."

"I can understand why Katrine liked him, but Roxanne?"

"I know what you're thinking; it's what everyone thinks until they get to know her. Roxanne is, or was, a real brain. She was smart; she wanted to do something great with her life like build buildings, sky scrapers... She had dreams. School wasn't even that hard for her, and boys, well, most of them were afraid to even touch her. She scared them all. But not Johnny. He liked that she was hard to get. He liked that she was smart and mysterious and kissed better than the others."

Susan smiled weakly.

"That – especially *that* really bothered me." She stroked her hair. "I mean, really, you like a girl better than another just because she's an excellent kisser? Johnny wasn't even that good looking, but he knew how to treat a girl, you know?"

Susan nodded.

"And I loved him. Loved... Well, that's in the past. What was I saying?"

"You were telling me a little about Roxanne and her sister."

"Yes. I mean, no two sisters could have been more different. They told stories about tricking the teachers and the boys, switching places, but most of us who knew them could tell them apart."

"And the drugs?"

"Katrine had been going off on them for years. Roxanne, she'd just started them as far as I know. After she and Johnny broke up it was almost like she didn't care anymore. About her future, you know. She just wanted to get high."

"Are you okay?" Susan asked.

"I am now, now that Oscar is in the picture. You really do have a kind son Mrs. James. By the way, does he know you came to visit me?"

"No. He's at home."

"Do you want me to keep quiet? I mean, do you think he'll get angry knowing you're here?"

Susan wasn't sure, but she figured he would be. She also knew something else far more important.

***

It was time to see Johnny, but Susan couldn't do it. She couldn't even look at herself in the mirror. Why was it always this way with her? And why hadn't Henry said anything this morning as she'd fixed his breakfast? Maybe he was worried over his own visit with the police, maybe he wasn't feeling as well as she figured. But she couldn't blame him, could she?

Stopping in front of the house, she tried to breathe in evenly. In just two days Katrine would more than likely be charged with murder, and her brain had just swung into high gear. She had to speak to these people, but she hadn't considered her son's feelings, not even for a moment.

What would he think? Say? Would he accuse her of going behind his back? Would he sit in shock vowing never to speak to her again? Well, one thing was for sure. She was letting her emotions swirl in her head like tapeworms.

Opening the car door, she got out and made her way to the door. Though her husband's car was gone, the door to the house was unlocked. Brianne had to be here, and if not, Oscar. She inhaled deeply and walked inside.

Oscar sat at the table as if expecting her. Brianne was somewhere else, but not in the kitchen. He held her in his gaze.

"Oscar, let me explain…"

Funny that his look would explain all, but so it was. As he stared at her she sat. She didn't speak and neither did he. She knew all the words that she needed to say but they wouldn't come out. She'd made a terrible mistake.

"Mom?"

She closed her eyes and opened them. "I'm sorry."

"So, you found out."

"I'm sorry. My detective instinct just clicked in. I…had to know some things."

"Don't you think you should have asked me first?"

"Yes, but…"

"No buts, Mom, especially not about this." She had never seen him cry. She was tired of seeing all of the crying, all of the emotion, all of the pain. "I should have told you myself that I've had drugs."

"What?"

He held up his hand. "Just let me talk. I have been going to parties like this for years. It started with drinking, and when the drinking wouldn't give me the fix I needed I started doing other things. I have been managing it for a long time, but… oh, Mom I'm so sorry!"

Oscar leaned in. She could smell the sweet scent of his breath. "I know I should have told you. You didn't need to go and see Matty. She knew everything, but you should have come to me!"

The room was a silent morgue.

"Your sister?"

"She doesn't know. She doesn't use, Mom, I made sure of it."

"Just like you made sure that she didn't take that sip of beer?"

Oscar looked down. "She only went to a couple of parties, I promise. She met Matty and she met Roxanne and she met Katrine. All of them. But she didn't use."

"What was she doing while you were using?"

A blank stare followed. "I don't know."

"And Matty, does she use?"

"No."

"You know that."

"She's been trying to help me. I'm sorry, Mom."

"Sorry doesn't begin to cover it. Where is Brianne?"

"In her bedroom. I told her I needed to talk with you about something."

"Get her."

Oscar stood and retreated down the hall. She watched after him, trying to slow her breathing, to fill her head with wise, loving words, but everything was in commotion. What had just happened? Hadn't she meant to apologize to him for sneaking around him instead of letting him know where she was going? Breathe in, breathe out, she told herself as she waited, and as their voices approached and Brianne sat down, Susan placed her hands on her eyes.

So, this was it. But how was she to know any of this? Had she seen any signs, anything that would direct her? Ms. Martha Boaz had had a drug problem. Why hadn't she seen the signs in her own son?

She looked up. Tears were falling from Brianne's eyes. "What is it, Mom? Am I in trouble?"

She touched her hand. "At the party, did you take any drugs?"

Brianne gaped at her. "Drugs?"

"Yes."

"Just that beer. Is that drugs, Mama?"

Brianne had never used the word, Mama, in her presence, ever. She sounded like a child, a small child.

"Beer isn't good, but I'm talking about illegal drugs."

"Illegal drugs?" She looked at her brother.

"You can tell her. She knows about me already."

"No, Mama, I have never used drugs." The words were muddled, almost whimpering.

"Good."

"Oscar is trying really hard to get off of them. Matty is helping."

"I know."

"And I've been helping too. I didn't want Oscar to go to the party. I tried to keep him home. He got mad but I just followed him out to the car and got in anyway."

"And Matty let you?"

"I don't think she knew what to do. Maybe she felt grateful to get some help."

"Why would a girl trying to help allow drugs at her party?"

"Her dad wasn't there. And besides, she didn't bring them. Katrine did."

"We'll need to talk to your father about this. Right now, he's at the police station speaking to someone about what we've recently learned, knowing that when he speaks, Katrine will be even further in the deep, dark hole than before. But he has to tell the police the truth. We all need to tell the truth."

That afternoon, when her husband returned home they were still sitting at the kitchen table. No one had even thought to eat.

Henry sat and took Susan by the hand. "So, what have we been discussing on this fine day?" he began.

157

OVER EASY

Stranger than Fiction

It wasn't enough that things were swirling faster than Susan could keep up with them. Henry had some news of his own.

"I went to the station and told them what we'd recently learned. They thanked me, and then had some words for me as well. Fred Cardigan has been found."

"I can't believe it."

"Believe it, Honey. The man was spotted going into Carly Petersen's place. He's being questioned even as we speak."

"And what of Carly?"

"The same. They're both at the police station."

"Gads. What a day!"

"Perhaps we need to have more of these family talks," Henry said, staring at his son. "I realize neither of you have had the best of upbringings, but we've got to be open and honest with each other from now on. Doing the police work that I do, I see lying, stealing, cheating and more, and I'd like to think our family is better than that."

"Sorry, Dad."

"We'll get you some help, would you like that?"

Oscar nodded.

"And Brianne. I'd like to see you make it through high school. Your grades are good, let's keep it that way."

"Okay."

"Susan?"

Susan looked up. It was her turn.

"I love you, do you know that? And I love it that you also love detective work, but perhaps it's time to step back a little, see the vision of what is happening, instead of jumping ahead unbarred."

"But I had plans to…"

"I saw the list and it frightened me a bit. Let me take over on Johnny. He seems a bit creepy to me. You can focus on Gretchen Conner, the jewelry lady. I find it fascinating that she has found her way into this investigation and that your friend, Jane Dove, brought about her entrance in sort of a roundabout way. I don't know how you do it, Honey – it's like you're a metal detector or something, but instead of dragging in metal, you drag in suspects."

"The more the merrier."

Everyone laughed.

"We've got one day to sort through everything and get some proof under our belts, before that poor little girl goes to court and brings her brother with her. We have 24 hours to find out once and for all who killed Roxanne Anderson. Is everyone in?"

***

After getting Gretchen's work address, Brianne came with her. Oscar was with Henry.

Gretchen lived on the west side of town where the houses were small and the crime visibly rampant. But she smiled at them from the threshold of her two-story home and showed them in to the kitchen. "Would you like some tea?" she asked.

The house was musty as an old trunk, but Susan smiled pleasantly in response. "Thank you, we would like that," she said.

After everyone had been served, Gretchen took a sip and returned the tea cup to its matching saucer. "So, you are searching for the killer of that young girl. And you think I might know something?"

Susan nodded.

"We were hoping you could help us to fill in some of the gaps of the day it happened."

"What would you like to know?" She took another sip, replacing the tea cup softly.

160

"Well, for one, we hear that you were watching a small boy at the time of the murder."

"A boy? Oh, yes. His name was Jimmy or something like that."

"Kent... Kenny?"

"Oh, yes. Kenny. He was a cute one. I shouldn't have done it of course. I knew Roxanne alright. She came to most of my events – loved my jewelry – but when she asked me for the favor I almost said no. I have felt funny about it ever since, especially since Roxanne was the girl murdered that night. I tried to keep Kenny from running off, but you know how boys are. I was helping some nice customers when he must have taken off. When I looked up he was gone."

"What did you do?"

"Well, I searched for him, of course. I was worried sick, but I couldn't leave my booth. I wasn't signed up to watch for shoplifters, you know. Leaving my booth just wasn't a choice I had. I couldn't leave my jewelry like that without anyone watching over it. Suddenly, a girl approached. She seemed frantic about something; it was as if she'd seen something scary. At first I thought it was Roxanne, that she had returned. But this young woman spoke differently, kind of haphazardly, and said that she was the boy's sister and that she'd seen him over here and had come to get him."

"Did you ever speak with the police?"

"The day of the murder, yes. But they only asked me if I'd seen anything, which, of course I hadn't, so they pretty much left me alone after that."

"And the girl?"

"Well, I was so grateful. The last thing I wanted was a little boy at my age to care for. I told her, 'Your sister was just here, and she left him with me.'"

"She said, 'Where did she go?'"

I pointed in the direction I'd seen her travel.

"The girl thanked me and left."

"Did she tell you her name?"

"No, but she seemed in a hurry. She was a bit teary eyed – I figured because she was worried over her brother – and seemed more interested in finally finding him than in speaking with me. When she left, I was relieved."

"She didn't say anything else? Tell you anything?"

No, she didn't say anything else, but she was in a hurry and so I let her go."

"What happened next?" asked Brianne.

"Oh, I went back to my work."

"I suppose you fix watches as well."

"No, why do you ask? Just jewelry."

Susan took a deep breath. "And then what happened?"

"Well, this other woman walked up. She was pretty anxious herself. She told me in no uncertain terms that I should have kept to myself. We're all here to work, she said, not take care of other people's children. I asked her who she was. She blinked at me. 'You don't know?'"

"I almost laughed right in her face. It was so obvious that she thought herself the boss of everyone and everything."

"I said, 'No. Who are you?'"

"I take care of the facilities here; my name is Veronica." She reached out her hand to me as if she expected that I should take it. I didn't."

Brianne laughed. "No kidding."

"She wasn't very nice, had this bossy way about her. I've been doing the *Halloween Bazaar* for years, even before Justine Commons ran it, and I know a thing or two about bossy people."

"So, who was in charge before Justine?"

"Oh, someone else equally bossy, kicked off the team so to speak. One of the shoppers was found dead near the woman's restroom I think. A man ran the place then… You seem surprised. The *Halloween Bazaar* has some interesting history. I'm surprised you never looked it up, being as you seem like detectives and all."

Susan was embarrassed. She knew about the old woman and the pacemaker; what she still mulled through was the previous owner of the establishment. And then it came. The ten years' factor hadn't come by someone exactly; it had been printed in the paper, a quote by Justine Commons. The *Halloween Bazaar* more than likely had been running for ten years, but she still didn't know anything about who had been running it before that.

"What was the man's name?" Susan asked.

"Like the tea?"

Susan nodded and asked again. "Who ran the place way back then?"

"He probably doesn't like people to know. I know I wouldn't. I see him sometimes, mopping up spills and fixing broken heating units. You know that place can get pretty cold when the heating unit doesn't blow. I don't speak with him. None of the old-timers do. He has a temper like a red-hot chili pepper."

Brianne shrieked suddenly, making the old woman jump. Susan, who was trying to be dainty with the cup, had just placed it to her lips, the liquid stronger now that she'd given it time to steep, when the shriek had erupted.

***

Henry had brought along Officer Crump. The rest of them, scrunched in the back of the police car, whispered amongst themselves.

"So, let me see if I understand this," Oscar began, not really looking at anyone as they drove, though Susan could see the wheels turning. "We have to get Cecil to confess. If he is the murderer, then everything else falls into place. That Fred guy, he may sell the drugs but he didn't kill Roxanne. He didn't have clear access to her. But Cecil did. He has access to the entire show, and he's the only one strong enough to pierce Roxanne's head in one try. Fred may not have been able to do it even if he wanted to.

"Someone entered that restroom. Someone who could come and go wherever and whenever they wanted to. Cecil could go in there, pretending to fix a toilet or the vanity mirror. I don't know. We didn't see him kill that girl but he must have; and someone must have seen him, someone who isn't talking, someone who is probably getting shut up with drugs: someone like Katrine. She saw it. Heck, she may have even known it was going to happen. Maybe she tried to stop it or maybe they were all in cahoots together. Roxanne was going to speak up, she'd tried to reach out after all to Brianne, but there were those who didn't want her to reach out – people like Fred Cardigan."

"And what of Veronica Edwards or Sadie Chartreuse? Brianne asked. "They could have been involved."

"Right." Susan's head whirled. "First, let's have a talk with Cecil. We can work our way down from there."

"Great idea." Henry sat in the front seat and Susan couldn't help but be proud of him. He sat straight up, eager to learn more. Minimal were the days when he slept all day and awoke just to eat or to take a short walk around the block. In just a short time he would be back to normal.

***

The place was dark when they reached it, a shadow of the grand place Susan had grown to loathe. What secrets did it yet hold? Well, they were about to find out.

As expected, Cecil's lone car sat in the parking lot. Hoping to go inside, she was quickly hushed. "Stay here, all three of you. Henry and I will investigate," said Officer Crump.

"What?" Oscar asked.

"You need to be here with the women. Keep them safe in case anything comes up."

"Like what?" Susan's knees were suddenly shaking.

"We don't know what we'll find in there. You need to be kept safe."

Perhaps it was no surprise, but Susan was still angry. This was the culminating point of their investigation; at any moment, the secret would be revealed. And she had to wait – outside?

"I know how you feel, Honey," but this is for the best. "Sit out in the car. Turn on the heater if you need to, but stay put."

"But…"

"Mrs. James, listen to your husband."

Oscar touched her arm. "Maybe they're right."

"Yes, maybe," Brianne whispered, taking Susan's hand. Her daughter's hand was moist.

"Okay, we'll wait, but be careful."

Henry nodded and together the two men made their way to the front door. Henry already had the key and they both let themselves inside easily. The place was dark. As Susan and her compatriots watched from the car she couldn't make out a thing. Time ticked by. Ten, fifteen, twenty minutes. The car was getting cold. She turned on the heater. She sat at the driver's side, her daughter next to her, her son in the back. There was silence and darkness and suddenly, a gunshot.

Instinctively, Susan unlocked the police car door and got out. She couldn't see anything but darkness. Oscar leaned out the door. "Get inside!" she yelled.

The door slammed but not before she heard another gunshot and another.

"I'm going in!"

"Not without me!" Oscar was suddenly at her side, his hand squeezing into her tender flesh. "Not without me you're not!"

"What about me!" Brianne screeched. "You can't leave me here!"

Suddenly, the outside lights of the building turned on, blasting through the grass and trees that grew nearer the front doors. Susan could see the sidewalk and three men emerging from the darkness.

"Maybe we won't have to," she said. The figures were dark. One of them was large; the size of the Officer, the other was of medium build – her husband. Yet another engulfed them all. He was walking out front, his wrists – cuffed.

As the men neared the car, Susan breathed a sigh of relief. No blood. So, what had the gunshots been about?

Henry answered her as if she'd raised the question. "Gave him a fright, I tell you," he said, pushing Cecil into the back seat. Oscar scrambled to the right so as not to touch him. Officer Crump followed, directing Cecil to the center back.

***

"It took some doing but Cecil had finally opened up. Sure, at one time he was the owner of Inglewood, all walls, nuts and bolts, but no more."

Henry smiled at his joke that wasn't very funny. Susan didn't laugh. They were sitting on the couch once again and Henry was looking tired. Still, the revelation was rewarding.

"There were some financial problems."

"Don't tell me. Fred," Susan said.

Cecil couldn't pay back the loan. In time, he also lost the business and all that went with it. He begged for a job. Fred wouldn't give it – it was always drug money even then, but he was hired on by Justine Commons, who I now know is not so common."

"Why is that?"

"Her father owns the place, and she gets all the just desserts she wants if you know what I mean."

"No, I guess I don't."

"Her position for one; she didn't even make it through college. She and Veronica are actually friends, can you believe it? She hired her on as top dog, even though she has no real experience, other than the fact that we'd all agree she likes to control people. Those two would do anything to keep this place."

"Like murder?"

"Perhaps, though Cecil said he didn't do it. He was there, of course. He saw Roxanne fall and heard the boy scream. He saw the hand reach out. Yes, he was hurting for money, he hated the fact that he no longer owned the place and that the folks who currently walked the premises were *lying fakes*. He knew that drugs were sold during the event, under the rug, in secret. He'd even bought some himself a few times just to take the load off, but he was a lowly cleaning man now. No one would believe him if he shared what was happening, and then he'd get fired. This was his only living, and who would hire an old man if he had to go out and look for work? You should have seen him, crumpled up and lost, confessing all of the times he'd sold to minors."

Susan was mortified. "Well, if it wasn't Cecil, who then? Are we actually back to Katrine?"

"I'm afraid so," said Henry.

***

Susan and Henry attended court, for support more than anything else. Sure, they had discovered some things the last few days, but not enough to convict anyone – unless one counted Katrine. Susan knew most of them in the room: Veronica Edwards, Sadie Chartreuse, Cecilia, even Mark. She watched Fred Cardigan from the corner of her eye, sitting up front, and nearby, Carly Petersen. She hadn't had time to speak with her – the last suspect on her list. But she was here now. They were all there, including Cecil just two rows in front of her, nearer the bailiff. Brianne had been forced to come; she'd been issued a subpoena, and Oscar had come to support Matty who had also been issued the same document.

The Andersons sat together near the front and behind their daughter, but they weren't speaking, though much of the room was. Katrine's head was bowed in front of her, and from the angle where she was sitting, Susan could see tears staining her cheeks. Her lawyer sat next to her, a round man with a suit coat and slick brown hair. She also spotted Officer Crump, leaning against one of the interior doors. Johnny was there, as was Justine Commons, of *True and Vine*. Even Gretchen was there. Was she making a necklace?

Susan felt winded even though she'd been sitting for the past hour. What was taking so long? The room didn't seem heated, though she knew it was, and Henry had nudged her more than once trying to keep her awake. Time was ticking and nothing was happening.

When the judge entered, a stiff, gray-haired man who sat in his chair like a frozen corpse, Susan almost laughed. He didn't even look – real. Looking around the room she must have been the only one to notice it; everyone else seemed fascinated. Suddenly, she could hear as well as feel breathing in the room, and wondered if everyone's heart pounded like hers was. Henry nudged her.

"Sorry," she whispered, not realizing until then that she'd stood up along with the rest of them when the judge had entered. "Be seated," he said now, and a rush of bodies sat almost in sync. Whispers ensued, and Susan looked once again at Katrine. She was still slumped over, her dark hair falling in straight lines down her back.

"How do you plead?" the judge commanded. His tone was firm and not the least bit sensitive. It made the hairs prickle on the back of Susan's neck.

Katrine stood, her head still bowed. The words came out softly. "Not guilty."

Commotion ensued, but the noise was quickly halted by the judge's gavel.

"Call the first witness."

Brianne stood. She walked slowly to the podium, her shoes clicking against the wooden floor. Susan had instructed her to wear a quieter pair; she'd been in courtrooms often enough to hear the clicking of feet, but the girl had been insistent. She was sworn in and sat, blinking her eyes quickly as if the tears were forthcoming.

Susan tried to catch her eye and smiled when her daughter looked her way. Everything would be okay, she'd promised her that.

"You knew Katrine?"

"Yes. And Roxanne." Brianne wet her lips. "I met them at a party."

"Tell me about the party."

"Okay, well, it didn't seem so bad at first. I spent a lot of my time with Oscar, my brother, and then he went to talk with Matty and so I was alone for just a little bit." She looked squarely at Susan. "I decided to make some friends. I walked over to Roxanne. She looked, well, sort of out of place there. She held a drink but she wasn't drinking it."

"What happened next?" The prosecutor scratched his head and placed his right hand in his gray jacket pocket.

"We talked for a long time. She told me all about her dreams to be an architect. She really loved buildings and told me someone was helping her to get into a special program. And then we talked about her family a little. She told me that she had a difficult time getting along with her parents – said they were real pushy about her getting great grades and all that. She also told me that her sister was causing her grief. They liked the same guy."

"Who was this…guy?"

"Johnny Reimbolt." She pointed to the third row.

"Anything else?"

"Well, Roxanne talked for a while about Johnny. She told me how much she liked him but that her sister was pretty mad when she found out. Katrine warned her that she'd better back off or else."

Susan took a deep breath, but it was hard to swallow. Brianne had never shared this piece of information with her, but it was obviously the reason the prosecution had decided to question her first.

"I felt really bad for Roxanne and told her if she ever needed someone to talk to that I was there for her."

The prosecutor smiled. "That's enough. Thank you, Brianne."

"You're welcome."

"Cross-examine?"

Katrine's lawyer stood. He wore a black suit, patent leather shoes, and a face that was all smiles. Peering down at Brianne, white teeth glistening, he asked: "And tell us, Brianne, did the time ever come for you to help Roxanne?"

"Yes. At the *Bazaar*." She smiled up at him. "It was fun at first. I was with my mom and her friend, Jane. I was looking at all sorts of stuff, when suddenly Roxanne was there. She handed me a note. I'd only met her that one time at Matty's house, and the room was pretty dark at the party, but something was wrong with her. Gads, she looked almost sick. She wore this beautiful black dress and she looked like she should go home to bed."

"Go on…"

"We talked for just a minute and then she hands me this note. She leaves me. A few minutes later I hear this loud scream. That's when I see her lying... dead."

"Did you see anyone nearby?"

Brianne was silent. Lots of people. My mom. Jane... "

"Katrine?"

"I object! Leading the witness."

"Sustained."

"Well, did you see anyone else you know?" The grin was even wider this time.

"No. Sorry. But I felt sorry for Roxanne. Really sorry."

When Brianne returned to her seat, she was still wiping away a tear.

"You did great." Susan patted her on the leg.

"Great." Henry leaned over and gave her a wink.

"Really? I felt like such a dummy..."

"Johnny Reimbolt?"

Johnny stood from his seat and walked to the front, trying to push down the hair he'd more than likely spiked that very morning. He frowned over at the prosecutor. Sworn in, he sat down, looking past the prosecutor to someone beyond him. Susan turned her head slightly to the left. Cecilia?

"Now, Mr. Reimbolt, how do you know the defendant?"

"We ah, dated?"

"For how long, Mr. Reimbolt?"

"About a year, but we – we didn't get along."

"Why weren't you getting along?"

"She – she was too jealous. Always harping at me for the girls I dated."

"And who did you date?"

"Lots of girls. I like girls."

"Be specific."

"It all started with Roxanne pretty much."

"So, you dated someone before Roxanne?"

"Well, yes."

"Objection, your honor! Whom Johnny dated before Roxanne has no bearing on this case."

"I will prove it does your honor."

"Proceed."

"Whom did you date before Roxanne Anderson?"

"Her sister, Katrine. We'd been dating for about a year, but no one knew that but us."

Susan breathed in and tried to calm her shaking hands. What kind of detective was she anyway?

"So, tell the court, Johnny, why the big secret?"

"I…well, Katrine and I were getting close. She thought I should date other girls to see if she was the right one. She was also supposed to date different guys, only she could never make herself do that. Once I started dating Roxanne, Katrine got real jealous. She told me to come back to her, but I really wasn't interested in doing that."

"Why not, Mr. Reimbolt?"

"Well, I…I had fallen in love with Roxanne."

"But you also cared for Katrine."

"Yes."

"So, what happened then?"

Johnny pushed down on his blonde hair, but it didn't stay. "Katrine started acting really strange. She and I got into lots of fights. She yelled at me all of the time. Then one day she told me that I had to stop dating her sister or…or she'd do something about it."

"What did Katrine say specifically?"

"I don't know… I mean….What did she say Mr. Reimbolt?"

Johnny grew pale. "She told me if I didn't stop dating her, that she would make sure that I did."

"Thank you, Mr. Reimbolt."

"Cross-examine?"

"So, Johnny, Mr. Reimbolt, how long have you known Katrine?"

"About five years, though we've only been dating for one."

"And you kept your dating relationship away from her twin sister for an entire year."

"Yes."

"That is hard to believe."

Johnny squirmed uneasily in his chair. "Believe it."

"So, when Katrine told you to stop dating her sister, what did you do?"

"Nothing."

"You did nothing, Mr. Reimbolt?"

"Well, I didn't stop dating Roxanne just because she asked me to."

"You didn't. Why not, Mr. Reimbolt. I thought you loved Katrine."

"Yes – and no. I mean, Katrine was a bit crazy if you know what I mean. Roxanne, well, she was more stable, more trustworthy, more, well…sane. I liked being around her and not just because she was a good kisser."

The court erupted into laughter. Even Susan had a difficult time not remaining quiet.

Johnny blushed. "I mean, so many people think that I'm this stupid guy who only cares about…well, I don't. I really wanted a good woman in my life. The problem was I found two and when Katrine threatened me it just did something to me. I made a choice."

"And what was that choice?"

"I chose Roxanne."

The court proceedings continued throughout the day, including testimony from Gretchen Conner who primarily spoke of boys who couldn't do what they were told – she was speaking of Kenny of course – and Justine Commons, who made it clear that she had every right to boss anyone around that she so chose. Wasn't she over the 'cleaning people'?

Nothing appeared to really be moving forward – that is, until after lunch.

Susan was walking back into the court room, arm in arm with Henry – Brianne and Oscar at their sides, when she heard it. Someone speaking:

"I can't believe Johnny lied about something so important. He loved me. There was no way he could have been dating Katrine for a year. Not even secretly. He was with me 24/7."

Susan stopped. A large partition separated her from the speaker. She motioned for Henry to stop and quickly shushed her children who were moaning about having to go back inside – though the moans primarily came from Oscar.

"So, why would he lie?" came the other voice. Suddenly, Oscar stood straight, no longer interested in going home, and Susan wondered if he was even breathing.

"I don't know, but it isn't fair, you know. I'm doing what I'm told. Why isn't Johnny?"

"Maybe he no longer cares about being force fed."

171

"I can't believe you said that. None of us are being force fed, whatever that means."

"Get a clue, Cecil! We have to keep doing what we're doing. We can't stop now!"

"We can stop if we want. Katrine will go to jail like we planned and we can continue to get the drugs."

"But not if Fred is in jail! Don't you see, we have to escape – now. We have to run!"

Oscar moved slightly to the right and Susan grew suddenly afraid. If he gave them away – now, everything was lost. She peered over at him, hoping against all hope that he'd be smart.

"Shhh, I think I hear someone. We'd better get back."

The voices moved away slowly, forcing her husband and children to walk to the right. When they were a fair distance away, only then did Susan speak. She looked over at Oscar. His eyes were bright with pain.

***

"We have to tell someone," Oscar blubbered.

"I know. I'll do it. You stay here with your dad and sister."

Brianne leaned down. "I knew there was something too perfect about her."

"Shut up."

"Sorry."

Oscar brushed at his eyes as Susan stood. "I need to catch him before he goes back into the court room. Maybe I can stand as a last-minute witness."

Henry nodded and Susan raced down the hall to the judge's chambers. She hoped he was there. She knocked. The door opened.

"Yes?" The old judge reeked of something. What, was it – Old Spice? He still wore his robes and they hung down his body like dried skin. What did the man weigh, 95 pounds?

"I – I have some last-minute evidence."

"You're that amateur detective, right?

Susan nodded. Now was not the time to squabble over sensitivities.

"Come in."

Stepping inside the room, Susan quickly realized they were alone.

"Sit," he instructed, waving his skeleton arm at a nicely cushioned chair across from his desk. She looked up at the clock. She had only five minutes.

Sharing all she knew, the judge grew silent. Susan stood, the sweat that had accumulated on her forehead more than likely making a mess of her makeup. "I appreciate the extra information," he said. "I'll pass it on."

"So, the trial will continue."

The judge shifted his gown. "Yes, though I will make the defense and prosecution aware of what you heard. You need to leave so that I can get that handled."

Susan rushed out. When she caught up with Henry and her children, they were already entering the courtroom. "Done," she said.

"Now what?" Brianne asked, her eyes tearing up.

"What?" Oscar echoed.

Henry looked at her wearily and squeezed her hand. Everything would be alright. It just had to be.

Antics

"I run a nice little clothing store," Fred began.

"That's not exactly true, is it, Mr. Cardigan?"

Fred began to finger the blue cardigan. "I mean, I used to have a clothing store. I sold all of my wares to Carly Petersen."

"The owner of *Holiday Hours*?"

"Yes."

"But doesn't Ms. Petersen run a Christmas store?"

"Y-yes," the man stumbled, "but I was in dire straits."

"And why were you in dire straits as you say?"

"It all started with the death of that girl. Everyone blamed me." He looked in the direction of Susan, his eyes glaring. "I – I got desperate."

"What did you do?"

"I ran off. I couldn't stand it. They'd – that detective woman and her family – found the evidence in my back dumpster."

"And the blood?"

"It was hers – the defendant's – the police said but I couldn't be sure."

"Of what, Mr. Cardigan?"

"That the death of that girl wouldn't still be pinned on me. But it was her – her I tell you!"

"How do you know that?"

"She was there – there right around the corner when her sister fell, yanking that boy out of the building. I saw her with my own eyes!"

Thank you, Mr. Cardigan.

"Your witness?"

"Isn't it true Mr. Cardigan, 'that girl' as you call her, the defendant, Katrine Anderson, knows you fairly well?"

The man smirked. "I suppose."

"And isn't it true she bought drugs from you, and that she'd been on these drugs for some time? Isn't it true that there were others, high school kids and college students who also purchased from you?"

"I don't know."

"Isn't it true that Roxanne came to you? She was one of your new clients and she was done with you – said she was going to tell everyone of the man you truly were?"

"No, that never happened!"

"Remember, you're under oath Mr. Cardigan."

"Isn't it true that the day in question came to a head because you'd finally, once and for all, discovered a solution to busy bodies like Roxanne Anderson?"

"I tell you, someone else killed that girl, and the murderer was her sister!"

"No further questions."

When Susan was called up she looked around the room and met the warm eyes of her husband. Brianne stared in her direction, surprised but fully aware of why she'd been called up. Her new evidence would more than likely open some doors. Oscar was silent. The tears had dried from his cheeks but he didn't look like himself – worry lines creased his forehead, and since the revelation in the hallway, he hadn't looked over at Mattie once.

"Mrs. James. Well, you've been involved in this investigation for quite some time haven't you? Let me just say that you seem to have a knack for individuals falling dead at your feet."

Laughter echoed off the high ceiling but Susan said nothing.

"Isn't it true that you also believe the evidence points to the defendant?"

"While that is true I…"

"And isn't it true that you've been interested in this case since the beginning? Putting your comments in, speaking with the police and others about something you are not trained to understand?"

"Badgering the witness!"

"Tell, us Susan, what it is you hoped to gain from this investigation?"

"To find the real killer."

"Where does the evidence lie?"

"While it is true that the evidence points heavily to Katrine Anderson, I cannot believe that she killed her sister."

"Not even in a fit of rage?" The prosecutor scratched his head.

"No."

"Why not?"

"I just can't believe it."

"Though the evidence points to her? Sample the blood-stained paper towel. Her fingerprints!" The prosecutor buttoned his gray jacket and, walking to a table, produced the shoes in a sealed bag, and the gray sweats, also bagged separately. For the first time the courtroom saw it in all its glory.

Susan was dumbfounded. Hadn't the judge told him everything? Why was he questioning her in this way if he knew that Cecilia and Matty were hiding information about their involvement in this case?

"It may be her fingerprints but I don't believe she killed her sister. There was someone else that wanted her dead."

"Like who?"

"Fred Cardigan," Susan said, pointing in his direction.

"Your witness," the prosecutor said.

"Mrs. James. I know the police have been very satisfied with the evidence you've provided. With your husband and children, you've helped in an amazing way with this case."

"Thank you."

"I know Katrine Anderson thanks you too." It was difficult, especially at that moment, but when Susan turned her eyes to Katrine she knew she'd done the right thing. The girl's eyes glistened and it was if she spoke to her without words. Sure, the girl had made some poor choices, broken the hearts of her parents, scarred the faith of her brother through her lying and cheating, but she could never murder anyone – and most especially not her sister.

"Tell us what occurred in this courtroom this very day," the attorney began.

There was an audible gasp and some movement, but Susan directed her eyes to the attorney.

"I heard, through a partition, two people speaking. They were talking about arranging things for Katrine. How Fred Cardigan had been feeding them drugs, how they were scared that he'd be put in jail and they wouldn't be able to get them anymore. They wanted to run away."

"And who were these people?"

"Cecilia Warren and Matty Slack."

"No! We didn't do it! It was Cecil!"

The courtroom erupted. "Order! Order!"

Cecil stood, tears dripping from his sad eyes. "It was me, but it was an accident, an accident!"

Susan covered her mouth. She looked across the room and into Katrine's eyes. They were staring back at her, unblinking, in disbelief.

Epilogue

It was almost as Susan had figured it. Through Cecil, Roxanne had been killed. Katrine had been set up because she was the most likely 'candidate' for the murder – she was emotionally charged over the boy she and her sister were fighting over and she was high on drugs much of the time. The chances were good that she wouldn't remember much of anything – especially if she got help to remember things a certain way.

Susan learned that Fred was indeed selling drugs to both college and high school students. Sure, he'd use the yearly event to sell, but this was sort of the party between them; the college cafeteria, Greenfield, was always a great place the rest of the year. Johnny had no idea what was going on with any of them, but *he was a great client* and Cecilia and Matty were of *great help as always.* Things turned sour when Roxanne wanted to improve her life. She wasn't yet selling, but she'd begun to use and wasn't yet 'clocked in' like the others. For Roxanne, the drugs were still 'social', she still didn't need them like the others, though things would change in time if he did things right. She had a *good head on her shoulders*, even Fred could see that, and *she should never have been approached, even with their united interest in architecture*; amazingly, he'd once had a high-profile architecture firm himself.

Still, *what's done was done.* Yes, the idea had come to him, the day of the *Halloween Bazaar*, how to *rid himself of her.* But he would need some *brute strength* to pull it off. Cecil was also *under his wing* so to speak. If Cecil killed the girl the man would be released from his meagerly duties. He would never have to work again.

Cecil was stubborn at first. He said he *didn't know Katrine personally*, but she was a young girl, not hard to manipulate. And he was able to do so, quite easily. He'd cover up for her; keep her free of jail time. She believed him kindhearted, sort of a valiant knight, and this *grieved him more than he could say*. He planted the evidence on the murder weapon, having used the paper towel to cover up his own fingerprints as he struck Roxanne. *She is standing up – groggily speaking. Katrine is weeping in the corner. She is holding the shoe with the fresh blood. He is consoling her. He is advising her to leave the restroom, to go home.*

But she doesn't go home. She washes her hands in the sink, and looks up at him *dreamy eyed*. She leaves the restroom and he doesn't know what to do. He tells her briefly, that he will take her to his car. She can *sit there safely* until he returns.

She doesn't want to do that. She goes into the main room.

The scene plays itself in Susan's mind. She can hardly believe what she's hearing:

I can't follow. I have to get rid of the shoe. I cover it with more paper towels and walk out the front of the building hoping no one notices. Most of them are in the main room. I leave the front and walk around to the back.

I see Fred. 'Where's the shoe?' he asks.

I pull it from around my back and hand it to Fred; he shoves it in a box in the back of his van, but I've been seen by someone. Sadie Chartreuse. She is picking up speed, coming to us, clipboard in hand.

What's up with you two, and why do you have blood on your hands? she asks.

I look down. The paper towel has seeped through.

Well?

Katrine. I saw her. I tried to help. She killed that girl.

You mean she murdered that young woman they just carted off?

Cecil's heart *dropped* – dropped every time he thought of what he'd done, he said.

As Susan sat in disbelief, the pieces began to click even more.

The *Halloween Bazaar* was merely a front for what was really happening. And it wasn't the only event where drugs were bought and sold like candy at a candy store.

Sadie wouldn't speak up about what she thought she knew, because she didn't want to lose the only hope of a grand future with plenty of money.

Justine Commons was a perfect fit. She kept her mouth shut. She and Sadie Chartreuse were the best of friends. For Veronica, 'free' goodies were her thing. None of them liked Fred Cardigan, but he had the stuff they needed.

Though Matty Slack and Cecilia Warren were not killers, they were definitely interested in the 'candy'. They helped to shield Cecil in the murder, Cecilia keeping interested onlookers at bay during the murder, and Matty, directing traffic in her own way as questions were asked and suspects prodded – she'd made the phone call to Fred. As for Mark Rand, he knew something was going on, though he hadn't yet placed a finger on the goings-on at Inglewood. Gretchen Conner was as innocent a woman as anyone could have been, with no clue as to what was happening right under her nose. Veronica Edwards was merely a temperamental cleaning lady and knew nothing about the plan, neither did *she want to*.

As for Carly Petersen, she really had no clue as to what Fred Cardigan was really about either. He'd helped her put up her store when she'd had no money, and had pretty much taken care of her for years. What did she give in return? Her love, shallow as it was. But that's all he'd wanted. Still, it wasn't enough in the end. She was getting tired of the charade and was ready to move on, but how could she walk away from a man who had helped her get back on her feet? How could she leave him stranded when he had no place to go and when everyone was looking at him as a murder suspect?

She *had to take him in*. She *had to take in his inventory*. It was the least she could do for all that he'd done for her.

Though the Andersons had never needed to get up on the stand; the expressions on their faces told Susan all she needed to know. As they held their son and embraced their daughter, it was all Susan could do to remain calm; still, the tears came unbidden.

Officer Crump was there in that moment, shaking her hand.

Susan smiled through her tears.

"It's crazy. Every piece of evidence was pointing to that girl."

"That's what you need to know about Susan. She has a knack for detective work. What you don't see on the outside is bundled up inside just waiting to escape."

Susan smiled. "What did Henry mean – exactly?" This case was definitely not 'over easy,' in fact it was about as 'scrambled' with suspects and as 'hard boiled' tough as she'd ever experienced. Still, she'd had the help of Henry and her daughter Brianne, and even Oscar, who had a way of taking things in stride even if his heart was more than likely breaking.

"Are you going to miss her?" she asked now.

Looking to the doors he watched as Matty was led away. She looked back only once, but the look wasn't friendly. Still, Oscar managed to squeeze Susan's hand. "Don't worry. She's beautiful all right, but I have a funny feeling there's someone better for me, someone who speaks the truth."

Susan wasn't sure who the new girl would be; she wasn't sure of anything really, only that she loved her husband and her children, and that life had a way of sorting itself out.

Katrine seemed not able to let go of her mother or father – though there would be a time she'd have to – at least when it came to working through drug therapy. Now, however, there were smiles all around, and it occurred to Susan that she'd done something right after all. After all of her bungling, her wrong turns, her plain out stupid sleuthing, she'd made it through this case practically unscathed.

She wished in that moment that Jane had been here to see this, but she'd been unwilling to attend the court proceedings. Still, she'd given Susan encouragement before leaving her. "You know, things have a way of working out. Know that my heart is with you..." Jane had touched the necklaces hanging around her neck, "...even if I can't be there personally."

As usual, they'd embraced upon parting and Susan had left feeling a bit lighter than when she'd arrived, hoping and praying that her friend knew something she didn't.

And she'd been right, about this at least.

All Susan knew for sure was that Henry was here and her children completed her life. Katrine would be able to return to her family, and the real culprits – Cecil, and the conniving Fred, would be placed in jail where they belonged.

Embracing her husband and children, Susan took one more look at Katrine, and the smiles that followed her all around. The courtroom was full of happy voices, pleasant handshakes and an endless supply of good wishes. With a peace in her heart not felt inside for months, Susan couldn't help but be completely pleased about how things had worked out. She opened the courtroom door. The day was waiting.

Eggs Benedict

Ingredients

> 6 Slices of ham or Canadian bacon
> 3 whole English muffins, you will have 6 sides
> 6 eggs poached or cooked "Over Easy."

Blender Hollandaise Sauce

> 10 Tbsp. Butter
> 3 egg yolks
> 1 Tbsp. lemon juice
> ½ tsp. salt
> Dash of Tabasco sauce

Melt the butter and set aside.

Put 3 egg yolks, a tablespoon of lemon juice, 1/2 teaspoon salt in the blender with the Tabasco sauce, blend on medium to medium high speed for 20-30 seconds, until eggs lighten in color.

Turn blender down to lowest setting, slowly dribble in the hot melted butter, while continuing to blend.

Transfer it to a container you can use to spoon the sauce on the Eggs Benedict.

While you are blending the Hollandaise Sauce:

Toast the English muffins in toaster or on broil in the oven.

Warm the ham or Canadian bacon wrapped in foil in the oven.

Poach the eggs by cracking one egg at a time into a pan of simmering water. Do not add a second egg until the first is almost done. Take out when done with a slotted spoon.

Assemble the first Eggs Benedict in this order.
>> English muffin
>> Ham or Canadian bacon
>> Poached or "Over Easy" egg
>> Generous portion of Hollandaise sauce

Enjoy!